BODYGUARD'S SAINT-TROPEZ TEMPTATION

BRYONY ROSEHURST

If you purchased this book without a cover you should be aware that this book is stolen property. It was reported as "unsold and destroyed" to the publisher, and neither the author nor the publisher has received any payment for this "stripped book."

Recycling programs for this product may not exist in your area.

ISBN-13: 978-1-335-47090-4

Bodyguard's Saint-Tropez Temptation

Copyright © 2026 by Bryony Rosehurst

All rights reserved. No part of this book may be used or reproduced in any manner whatsoever without written permission.

Without limiting the exclusive rights of any author, contributor or the publisher of this publication, any unauthorized use of this publication to train generative artificial intelligence (AI) technologies is expressly prohibited. Harlequin also exercises their rights under Article 4(3) of the Digital Single Market Directive 2019/790 and expressly reserves this publication from the text and data mining exception.

This is a work of fiction. Names, characters, places and incidents are either the product of the author's imagination or are used fictitiously. Any resemblance to actual persons, living or dead, businesses, companies, events or locales is entirely coincidental.

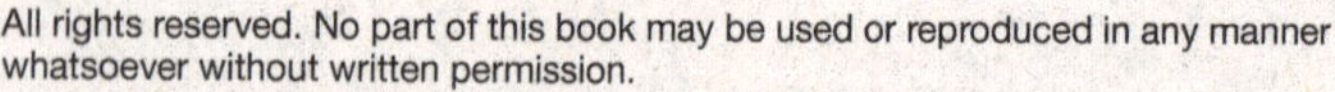

For questions and comments about the quality of this book, please contact us at CustomerService@Harlequin.com.

TM and ® are trademarks of Harlequin Enterprises ULC.

Harlequin Enterprises ULC
22 Adelaide St. West, 41st Floor
Toronto, Ontario M5H 4E3, Canada
www.Harlequin.com

HarperCollins Publishers
Macken House, 39/40 Mayor Street Upper,
Dublin 1, D01 C9W8, Ireland
www.HarperCollins.com

Printed in U.S.A.

1 2 3 4 5 6 7 8 9 10 HDC 28 27 26 25

Her pinkie finger prickled, a zap of energy crawling up her arm, and she opened her eyes to see Dani's hand beside hers on the railing.

She still faced the party, and didn't look at Sasha at all, but she was there. Comforting her.

Something tugged at Sasha: the urge to close the gap between them, bury herself in this new, unexpected safety.

Dani's finger twitched against hers, just once, and then she pulled away, and Sasha remembered that she wasn't a friend, and she certainly wasn't a soft place to land. She was here because Sasha had paid her to be here, and really, that meant she was the same as everyone else.

Except she didn't *feel* like everyone else as Sasha continued to endure that night's socializing. The opposite. If the lines blurred, it was because Sasha needed them to. She needed someone she could trust, and Dani Sharpe was the closest thing to it.

When the silhouette of the Saint-Tropez coastline returned to view, Sasha could finally breathe. She'd made it through the night, and she'd never have to see these people again.

Dear Reader,

I have always adored the romance genre for its joyful tropes and emotional exploration, so the opportunity to create *Bodyguard's Saint-Tropez Temptation*, my first Harlequin novel, has been a true privilege—especially as it means getting to bring more sapphic stories into the world!

It's no secret that the bodyguard trope is my favorite for all of the high stakes and forced proximity it offers, and I hope you fall head over heels with our reserved, butch protector! Dani and Sasha's opposites-attract dynamic is especially exciting because, at heart, they are both battling with the same loneliness and insecurity, even if the sources of their hurts are largely different. Similarly, exploring the personality and potential struggles of a celebrity feels particularly interesting, not just because it allows for the luxurious, sunny European settings Dani and Sasha travel to, but also because we see these issues play out on our screens every day with real figures. Peeling back the layers of a gruff, grieving northerner and a Hollywood starlet was as much of a journey for me as it was for the characters, and I hope you find something you identify with in their story.

Bryony x

Bryony Rosehurst is a Manchester-based romance author dedicated to telling diverse stories of love and happily-ever-afters—and perhaps a little bit of angst sprinkled in for good measure. She also hosts the queer podcast *Swords & Sapphics* with her long-distance best friend, Ivy. Under the name Rachel Bowdler, she has written *Honeymoon for One* and *Summer at the Scottish Castle*, and, more recently, *Kindling* and *Kiln Me Softly* under the name Bonnie (B.B.) Woods.

Bodyguard's Saint-Tropez Temptation
is Bryony Rosehurst's debut title for Harlequin Romance.

Visit the Author Profile page at Harlequin.com.

CHAPTER ONE

DANI SHARPE'S FIRST impression of Saint-Tropez? It was far too bright. Having grown up in the dreary English rain in a damp council house in Leeds, she was used to red bricks and *a lot* of puddles. France, it seemed, was without both of those things, at least this far south. She peered through the tall iron fence spanning the vast film-studio lot to behold sun-drenched buildings woven across the hilly terrain, painted in shades of peach and gold. More of them clustered below like pennies spilling over the coastline, highlighting the bustling town. Somewhere, a splash of green marked the ivy-covered hotel where Dani had slept last night, or tried to, but, even with her sunglasses on, she couldn't see it for squinting.

'Well,' she muttered, gazing towards the sparkling turquoise marina in the distance, 'you're not in Kansas any more, Dan.'

In fact, she wasn't sure she was in the same universe. In her black shirt and tailored trousers—which were just a smidge creased from being tugged out of her suitcase hastily this morning—

she was an inky blot in a sea of lush pink shrubbery. Even the huge car park she currently stood in was more like a Hollywood set, lined by tall palm trees swaying in the breeze. A block of trailers was stationed by the glossy offices, reflections of clear sky bouncing off the glass walls.

In this new career, she was used to feeling out of place among wealthy clients and strived not to let it bother her. They weren't better than her just because they had money, after all. Couldn't be if they relied on her to keep them safe for their extravagant events.

But now, it was difficult not to be a little intimidated. More so considering she hadn't had her usual briefing about the client beforehand. Her boss, Marcus, had warned only that Dani had been hand-picked by an extremely high-profile client, so she'd better be on her 'A game'.

The thought of Marcus and his excruciatingly high standards had her checking her watch: 12.54.

Thankfully, she hadn't parked too far from the offices, and it wasn't hard to miss her destination wedged between a long row of studios and production facilities. Huge silver lettering labelled the front of the building: Riviera Production Conference Suites.

She unrolled her sleeves and slipped her blazer on, shaking out her shoulders in an attempt to release the nervous tension. It didn't work, probably because her body knew what her brain was trying to ignore: she didn't deserve this. Sure, she'd worked hard to excel at this job, but she'd also chosen it to escape the failures of her life in Yorkshire. Every fancy location was a sharp poke to her ribs, every ray of sun a quiet whisper that said, *You shouldn't get to be here.*

Her legs carried her forward anyway, even as her chest grew tight. She gave a terse nod to the stone-faced security detail at the entrance, slipping off her sunglasses and hooking them over her pocket.

A set of sliding automatic doors brought her into a well-air-conditioned lobby that smelled like fresh wood and coconut suncream. The soles of her chunky brogues squeaked against the shiny mosaic floor as she strutted over to the front desk. Behind it, a younger woman who didn't deign to look up at Dani typed on her keyboard at a leisurely pace.

It had bothered her at first, the way these people treated her, as though money equalled superiority. Maybe it was her short, dyed red hair that gave her away, or her complete inability to tolerate make-up, or maybe it was that Dani would never, ever be one of them, no matter how she looked.

Maybe they sensed, too, that she didn't belong.

Either way, she was good at veiling her own insecurity, so she straightened her spine to reach her full five-foot-eleven height and cleared her throat with assertion. 'I'm Dani Sharpe with the Stars Protection Group. A client is expecting me.' She flashed her Stars ID from her pocket, which held the same pasty photograph as her passport. It had been updated only last year, but she barely remembered sitting in the photo booth, or filling out the application forms. Everything from that time was shrouded by the fog of a grief that still lingered. Sometimes, it was a comfort to fall back into it. Surrendering to it at least meant feeling close to the woman she'd loved and lost, and she surely deserved the suffering that accompanied her memory.

The receptionist barely glanced up from the computer. 'Third conference room on your left.' She waved faintly to the adjacent corridor and then went back to typing.

'Cheers.' *For nothing.*

Dani headed through another set of doors, where a wide, airy corridor yawned out for miles. Photographs and movie posters hung on the walls in golden frames, some featuring romantic French films she'd never heard of, others with English titles she vaguely recognised from nights spent scrolling through Netflix.

When she arrived at the third door on the left, she took a deep breath before knocking.

'One moment!' a small voice came from the conference room, followed by echoing footsteps.

When the heavy, grey-panelled door opened,

Dani wasn't all that surprised to find a gorgeous woman on the other side. She was younger than Dani had expected, but otherwise fitted the Hollywood mould to a tee. Blonde waves, a fresh, sun-kissed face and glowy skin without a trace of imperfection. She seemed nervous, shifting on the threshold, which bolstered Dani's confidence, though she did wonder if she'd got the wrong room. Most young clients gravitated towards the beefy male bodyguards for obvious reasons, especially for personal and long-term roles. It wasn't often that Dani was requested in their stead.

As Dani opened her mouth to introduce herself, their gazes locked and she forgot what she'd been about to say. The woman's eyes were the colour of the sparkling sea outside, pupils lined with a hint of deep green. Had Dani ever seen eyes that bright before?

Of course she had. She was probably suffering from sunstroke, or maybe it was just the effect of this place.

She gathered her composure, holding out her hand. 'Hi. I'm Dani Sharpe from Stars Protection Group. I believe you were expecting me.' She tried not to make it a question, which was easy given her naturally monotone voice.

The woman nodded, her hands clasped in front of her. She wore an apricot-coloured dress—likely designer, but Dani wouldn't know—patterned with delicate florals, exposing the arch of her collarbone. The pleated linen draped over wide hips before stopping midway down her golden thighs. She was both curvier and shorter than most celebrities Dani was familiar with, which might have been refreshing if her face weren't so heavily caked in bronzer, mascara and all the other cosmetics Dani paid little attention to. At forty-one, she probably could have done with make-up to conceal the creases slowly deepening around her eyes, but she hated the feeling of anything on her face, especially with the stifling summer heat outside.

Finally, the client must have realised that Dani was waiting and straightened up. Their palms collided, her cool, soft skin the perfect balm for Dani's hot, calloused hands. Sparks tingled along her knuckles, igniting a layer of static that made her more fidgety than usual.

'Right. Yes, Dani. Good to meet you!' her new client said, with an enthusiastic shake. Her voice was high, musical almost, her accent a clean southern British. Posh, in other words. Another thing that wasn't surprising.

'And your name?' Dani tilted her head, unable to contain her dry smirk. Clearly, this woman was used to being recognised, and it satisfied Dani to be the exception. Her job was in protection, but a few of her clients might do well with a bit of humbling on the side. She was more than happy to provide that—in a professional manner, of course.

'Oh, sorry!' The woman's throat bobbed, and she brushed her wispy fringe from her eyes. Her other hand was still in Dani's, and Dani didn't know why. 'I'm Sasha. Sasha March.'

Finally, Sasha pulled away, her hand falling limply to her dress. She stepped aside on high-heeled wedged sandals, with torturous-looking brown leather straps. Dani hadn't thought people—or adults, at least—still painted their toenails, but hers were an alarming shade of neon coral.

Dani pretended she wasn't looking at them as she headed in, pulling out a seat for herself and then one for Sasha. 'Shall we?'

'Yes. Thank you.' Sasha smoothed down her dress and slipped into a chair, smacking her shiny pink lips together as Dani took the seat adjacent. The sudden waft of fruity perfume caught her by surprise; made her want to draw closer for some reason. It wasn't light and playful, like most fragrances, but reminiscent of rich cherries and heavy syrup.

She had to remind herself that this was a client. One who was her polar opposite, no less. If she smelled like dessert, it was not Dani's job to notice.

But it was strange she had. Not much had penetrated through that fog of loss recently. Most days, she seemed to walk without even noticing her legs moving or her surroundings changing.

Always on autopilot, as if part of her were still underwater with Eve.

With just a conference table spanning the length of the room, their little corner suddenly felt too close, too intimate, especially when Dani adjusted her legs and found her knee grazing Sasha's. More static radiated up her thigh, lingering even when she cleared her throat and shifted away. God, she needed to get herself together. She wasn't usually this nervous, and Sasha March certainly wasn't the first pretty woman she'd worked for. Then again, she didn't usually receive an hour lecture from Marcus about how important this client was before the trip had even begun. Between that and finding herself in one of the most luxurious regions in Europe, her sun-addled mind was scattered.

Since it became clear that Sasha wasn't going to begin, Dani sat back and tried to refocus. She'd made it here. Now she had to find out exactly what Sasha needed her for.

'So, where should we start, Miss March?'

CHAPTER TWO

SASHA DRIED HER clammy palms on her dress, her stomach clenching yet again. It had been jittery since the moment Dani had knocked on the door. When she'd contacted the protection group's director, Marcus, she hadn't realised how vulnerable it would make her feel to sit here and confess to a stranger that she needed help.

Of course, it didn't help that the stranger was tall, dark and the perfect mix of handsome and beautiful. The grainy passport ID on Dani's Stars profile hadn't done justice to the real thing. Sharp, high cheekbones, deep red hair shaved on one side and broad shoulders barely contained by the fabric of her black blazer. Dani's file stated she was forty-one, and that maturity bled through in the form of confident ease and unshakable poise, as well as a couple of evident scars. One across her eyebrow, another on the cleft of her chin. It made Sasha wonder how many things she'd survived in her life. Working for wealthy clients must have been easy in comparison to whatever had left those marks. Was that why she'd received an award for police bravery?

For a moment, Sasha considered dropping the whole thing. What if she'd made a mistake? What if she was being overdramatic?

What if she'd regret it all?

But then she thought of what would come after. Going back to work as though everything were fine. Signing a contract for a seven-movie franchise that would leave her suffocating for another ten years. Working with her ex-husband, Tom, every day, unable to go and buy so much as a coffee without being spotted, only to end up in a hotel room alone with no one to call, no one to keep her grounded, while unflattering photographs and malicious gossip were splashed all over social media. It was unbearable. Even more unbearable than sitting here and trusting a stranger. She needed change. Now.

But first, she needed her throat to stop feeling so dry.

'Would you like a drink?' Sasha offered, motioning to the tray of water and orange juice in the middle of the table. The ice cubes were already melting despite the building's air conditioning, condensation beading down the pitchers.

'Yeah, please. Water's good.' Dani's vowels were soft, northern. It was disarming to hear a regional British accent after months of listening to an eclectic mix of American and European ones, especially with Dani's gravelly tone. If Sasha remembered her Stars profile correctly, Dani had been on the West Yorkshire police force, one of the reasons why Sasha had chosen her. Compared to the other candidates, a predominantly male line-up, she'd looked the most…real, Sasha supposed. She'd felt more inclined to trust Dani, and not just because she was a woman. Her brown eyes and quiet confidence promised reliability, her roughness a much-needed contrast to the superficial beauty Sasha faced every day. She'd needed different, and Dani was precisely that.

Maybe too different. It was hard to find any warmth at all as Dani surveyed her. She wasn't intimidating, but she wasn't friendly, either. More detached, something Sasha wasn't used to after years of fame. People knew who she was and wanted to insert themselves into every aspect of her life. They either loved her or hated her, but never did they simply not care.

The air pulsed around Sasha suddenly. Maybe she'd made the wrong choice, picking someone with so much experience. She'd thought it would help her cause, but now she wondered if it would only make her seem even more ridiculous. For some reason, she hated the idea of seeming ridiculous in front of Dani.

Pushing the thoughts away, Sasha slid the tray of beverages over to them and hoped Dani didn't notice her hands shaking when she poured water into two tall glasses.

'Cheers.' As Dani tipped the glass to her lips, her sleeve fell to reveal the hint of a curling tattoo, its edges covered by a leather watch. Sasha wondered what it might be: something dark and intense, or something surprisingly delicate?

'How was the trip here? Not too long, I hope,' Sasha said after a long swig of water. She had no idea if it was adequate small talk, but she was trying. That had to count for something.

'I don't mind a long drive.' Dani shrugged, using the pad of her thumb to wipe away a droplet of water that hadn't reached her mouth—quite a feat, since her lips were perfectly plump. Not that Sasha noticed. Much.

'Good!' She brightened, and then, observing Dani's alarm, retreated back into herself. 'That's good.'

Hell, she was getting ahead of herself. She'd never planned anything secretive before in her life, and, so far, she was failing miserably at it.

At the sound of footsteps in the corridor, Sasha tensed. Her agent, Gabriella, was probably already on the hunt for her, and she could do without questions. She let out a breath when the footsteps passed straight by the door and continued on.

Dani watched, curiosity tugging on her brow.

'How about we start with why you hired a bodyguard?'

'Yes, okay.' Sasha sat up straighter, rearranging her fringe before it fell into her eyes again. She hated it, but her director, Rafael, had been insistent that Sara Chase *needed* bangs. Clearly, he'd never met a real woman before, because she doubted an FBI agent who spent her days chasing dangerous criminals had time to style her hair between the combat and pursuits. Not unless she also turned out to be a superhero, which wasn't in the script.

'I've had a lot of trouble with paparazzi and fans recently. Not *my* fans,' she added quickly. At the questioning cock of Dani's head, she elaborated, 'I recently went through a divorce, and the media spun the story to make me look like the bad guy. My ex-husband is also an actor, and he has *a lot* of terrifyingly loyal fans who are very angry with me for things I didn't actually do.'

It sounded absurd to say out loud. Most celebrities had trouble. Many dealt with invasions of privacy on a regular basis. She wasn't the first woman to suffer at the hands of the media, and she wouldn't be the last.

But this wasn't the life she'd signed up for.

If Dani thought her melodramatic, she didn't show it, instead nodding slowly. 'I see. Have any incidents occurred where you felt that you were unsafe?'

Sasha shook her head, but then winced at the memory of the airport a few weeks ago. France had greeted her with a bombardment of fans demanding photographs, videos, autographs. When Sasha had tried to explain that she was exhausted from the flight—and she hadn't wanted her pasty, make-up-free face to be immortalised on the Internet—the group had transformed into a mob of angry protestors. Airport security hadn't been able to get her away quickly enough. All she remembered were bodies closing in on her like walls, hair ripping from her scalp, clothes getting torn as they'd fought over her like wolves over a scavenged meal. She'd barely heard the cruel shouts over all the mayhem, but they'd echoed in the silence of her hotel room for hours after. The very people who had begged her for selfies and attention had suddenly decided they hated her, because Sasha hadn't given them what they'd wanted.

Gabriella had only joked, *That's show business, darling,* and promised to arrange extra security before her next flight, so now it was instinct to water the experience down. 'I mean, they can get a little forceful. I've had a few coffees thrown in my face here and there, but nothing too drastic.'

'Sounds drastic to me. Certainly more than you should have to put up with. Is there a reason you don't already have a team in place? It seems unusual, in my experience, for somebody in the public eye to go this long without.'

'My agent usually arranges security detail for events, but…' Sasha paused, unable to tell the truth: that she needed somebody disconnected in every way from the people around her. 'It just felt like the right time to hire a personal bodyguard,' she finished cautiously.

'How about your current accommodation? Any security breaches there?' Dani's voice softened, and she leaned forward, fingers tapping the glass table between them. Sasha's chest fluttered, both with the proximity and the fact that Dani hadn't brushed her off. It had been a long time since anybody had taken her seriously.

'No, not while I've been here. I'm staying in a private villa, though. It's all gated and monitored.'

'Well, that's something. Still, it might be useful if I take a look around to make sure.'

Sasha worried at her bottom lip, tasting the bitter perfumed flavour of her designer gloss. This was where she was supposed to tell Dani the *real* reason why she'd hired her, but she still felt reluctant. Was still waiting for Dani to laugh in her face.

Then again, she didn't have much time to waste.

'You could, but I don't plan to stay here for much longer.' Sasha whirled a golden ring around her middle finger nervously.

'Ah. You're about to wrap up on set, or…?'

'Actually, no.' Finally, she lifted her eyes to meet Dani's. 'But I don't plan on working another day.'

Dani frowned. 'I'm not sure what you mean, Ms March.'

'I mean…' Sasha opened her mouth. Closed it. Smacked her lips together again as she considered how to say it. If she really wanted to. Her heart felt like a balloon about to pop. For weeks, she'd been considering this. Convincing herself that she couldn't possibly give everything up, only to find herself miserable when she returned to set. There were always hands on her—Gabriella's, Tom's, Rafael's. They made her want to crawl out of her skin. She lived with a heavy stone of anxiety in her gut, a knowledge that everybody surrounding her did not have her best interests at heart, and she couldn't take it any more.

The decision had been made, whether she chose to acknowledge it or not.

She planted her elbows on the table, their arms almost touching. She could feel the space between them like a tangible thing. A gap bursting with atoms she wasn't usually aware of, thousands of them dancing with electricity. When she wondered why, Sasha tried to explain it away as desperation: she needed Dani's help, and her skin and bones knew it.

She kept her voice low, just in case somebody

lingered outside. 'I need to leave…' She didn't know what to call her. Followed Dani's lead and went with, 'Miss Sharpe.' Hated how clumsily it rattled on her tongue. She'd rehearsed this conversation over and over again, yet none of it was going to plan.

'Dani,' the bodyguard corrected. 'Call me Dani, if you'd like.' Sasha's words must have registered, because she dipped her head in curiosity. 'What do you mean, you need to leave?'

That question was all it took for Sasha's long-held dam to finally burst. 'I don't want to be here. I don't want to keep filming this movie. I don't want to be photographed when I'm just trying to buy groceries. I don't want to go to yacht parties or see my name on every gossip site. I don't want to be clawed at like I'm prey when I get off a plane. I don't want to look at my cheating ex-husband's face every day. I want to leave, but they wouldn't let me break the contract. They want me to sign on for seven more movies. That's ten years of my life.' Her voice grew thick with tears. 'So I need to be discreet about it. I *need* to disappear before they can stop me. Do you understand?'

'Not even a little bit,' Dani retorted—but she didn't pull away, didn't break their closeness with the scoff Sasha expected.

'Look, I know how I must seem.' She *seemed* desperate, expression pained and voice squeaky, and she knew it. Hated it. But every day, it was harder for Sasha to keep going. Every day, forcing herself to live a life that wasn't hers any more hurt. She didn't know how to say that without sounding ungrateful, but she tried. 'But I'm… I'm exhausted. Have you ever been exhausted? So exhausted that you want to collapse somewhere and never wake up?'

Dani's breath caught in her throat, or maybe it was just the chugging air vent. Sasha couldn't be sure. Still, the scars on her face said that maybe she'd understand. Sasha *needed* her to understand.

'Tell me again what you're asking of me,' Dani ordered.

Sasha didn't dare miss a beat this time. If she'd been unsure before, she wasn't now. Finally voicing it aloud had sealed her fate, and she would do this with or without help. 'I'm asking for you to help me get out of here. To take me somewhere where nobody knows my name.'

When Dani only blinked, speechless, Sasha folded her hands over Dani's. She felt pathetic, begging like this, but there was no one else in the world left to help her. To everyone else, she was Sasha March. She had a job to do, people to impress, a role to play. Dani was a clean slate. She hadn't even known Sasha's name. 'Please, Dani. Say you'll help me.'

'I don't know if I can,' admitted Dani, removing her hand to scratch her chin slowly. Sasha tried not to wince at the show of rejection. 'Aren't there rules? Wouldn't breaking a contract get you in serious trouble?'

'I'm working with a lawyer to find my way around that. Honestly, right now, I don't care. I just need to get out. I'll figure the rest out later.'

Dani looked as if she wanted to curse. 'Okay, well, there are probably rules on my end, too.'

'I read over our contract more than once. I know there isn't anything stopping you from doing this. Bodyguards go on vacation with their clients all the time, don't they?'

'Yes, but you're not talking about a vacation. You're talking about actually running away.' Dani shook her head. 'Have you *really* thought about this?'

Anger boiled over in Sasha, splashing over her face, her cheeks, like scalding water. 'Of course I have!' she exclaimed with a hint of bitterness. 'And I chose you because, out of everyone, I thought maybe *you* might understand!'

Dani snapped back in surprise. 'Why would *I* understand?'

'You went from working with West Yorkshire Police, winning this huge award, to suddenly working for a European protection group with VIP clients. There must have been *some* kind of reason for the change!'

Sasha had thought that maybe an award in policing had spurred more attention for Dani, more than she'd been willing to bear, a little like her. She hadn't looked into it, more interested in that huge leap from one country to another, one career to the next. She had seen herself mirrored in it.

Once, she'd been a singer confined to grotty pubs in Kent, or busking on the street. Being noticed had been the beginning of her ruin, especially when she'd made the move to LA to record the second album. The more her popularity had grown, the more trapped she'd become. Most people might view fame as something sparkly, exciting and wonderful, but Sasha had learned it was anything but. It was lonely and restrictive and she had lost herself in it completely. She had no friends around her, nobody who cared about who she was when the spotlight dimmed. She didn't even know where her old, beloved guitar was any more—an instrument that she'd treasured, an intrinsic part of her, gone for ever.

Dani's jaw ticced, and she scooted back to put more space between them. 'Yeah, there was,' she answered slowly. 'The pay cheque.'

Sasha wanted to cry, feeling an invisible wall rising between them. Dani didn't get it. Sasha had been wrong about her, as she was wrong about everything.

She followed that roiling anger, because there wasn't much else left. The world had abandoned her. This was her last resort, her desperate plea for help, and it was being met with…nothing.

Her chair legs screeched as she stood up, strutting over to the window so she could turn her back to Dani. Outside, it was sunny as ever. The world was still turning, and Sasha was sick of it. She wanted it all to stop. 'You know, I don't have to explain myself to you. This is my life, and I've made my decision. I'm only asking you to do your job. If you can't, I'll find someone who will.'

In the window's reflection, Dani raked her short hair out of her eyes, then ran her hands along the rough buzz cut beyond her side part. She looked as though she regretted ever coming here, and Sasha couldn't keep her shoulders from sagging. Dani wasn't going to do it.

'Is there an option to get back to you on this?' asked Dani.

'I'm leaving tomorrow, whether you're with me or not.' She'd decided that this morning, right after Gabriella had asked her to sign the ten-year contract. Right before her director, Rafael, had announced a party was to be held on his yacht tonight, another unnecessary social event that Sasha couldn't stomach, one that would no doubt end in Tom drunkenly demeaning her in some way. She'd have to show her face if only to avoid suspicion, and at least it would give her some idea of whether Dani was truly capable of guarding her.

'But in the meantime, you'll accompany me to a party this evening.' She turned around, her gaze unwavering. Her sudden authority came as a surprise, even to her. Likely to Dani, too, because she kicked out her legs and observed Sasha as if she were an animal Dani wasn't sure would bite.

Good. It was about time she used her teeth. She was tired of people expecting only meekness and subservience from her.

Dani's breath swept across the conference table as she finally nodded. 'Okay. A party, I can do.'

CHAPTER THREE

As Dani stood up, the backs of her knees damp with sweat that had nothing to do with the climate, the door opened behind her. By the window, Sasha trembled before reassembling her mask. With pursed lips, she scraped the smudged mascara under her eyes and fluffed up her hair—just in time for a dark-haired woman to march in with an iPhone clutched in her hand. She tutted in Sasha's direction.

'*There* you are! I've been looking for you everywhere.' Like Sasha, the intruder spoke with a British accent, although hers was diluted by an American twang. Her near-black eyes snagged on Dani and she raised a brow. 'Who's this, then? New assistant?'

Dani fought not to roll her eyes. Did she *look* like an assistant?

Sasha, thankfully, didn't leave Dani time to wonder if she was supposed to answer. 'This is Dani Sharpe. She's my new security detail. Dani, this is my agent, Gabriella.'

'Nice to meet you,' Dani said politely.

Gabriella ignored her in favour of a laugh, smoothing a manicured hand through her straight chestnut highlights. 'Darling, if you wanted a bodyguard, you only had to ask.'

Dani didn't miss the way Sasha gulped. She inched slightly closer in a show of solidarity. Maybe she was hesitant about Sasha's little escape plan, but it was still her job to watch her back, and Dani got the feeling that Sasha's agent was part of the problem. On the outside, she appeared lovely enough, with a wide, perfectly straight grin, but condescension serrated her saccharine voice, enough to make the back of Dani's neck prickle with discomfort.

Sasha handled it better than Dani would have, forcing a pleasant smile. 'I found myself capable of hiring someone myself this time, but thank you.'

'Hm.' Gabriella narrowed her eyes. 'Well, are you capable of signing that contract? Because the executives are already getting antsy.'

Sasha bristled, expression darkening in the same way it had earlier when she'd talked about her fans. 'I told you I need time to think about it.'

Dani couldn't pretend to get it, all this movie-star nonsense. There was no job on earth that was worth the kind of treatment Sasha had hinted at—and yet, wasn't it what she'd signed up for? She clearly enjoyed the luxurious side of fame: the dresses, the make-up, the hair. Dani doubted

Sasha would survive a day without a salon, and what would come next? Nobody could hide for ever.

And yet something tugged Dani closer still, until her arm brushed Sasha's. She wasn't sure if she'd intended it to or not, only that Sasha seemed to soften at the touch. It was enough to settle some of the restless tension inside her. That need to help people had always been there, but it had dulled since losing Eve. She hadn't been able to save the woman she loved, and, in her eyes, it made her incapable, unworthy. This position was her final attempt to fool herself into believing that she hadn't become a complete waste of space.

Gabriella seemed oblivious to the souring atmosphere. 'Yes, darling, but most people only need a couple of hours to *think about* a multi-million-dollar deal.' She air-quoted *think about* with her free hand as though the concept was childish. 'The sooner you sign, the sooner we both get paid.'

Sasha's mask began to slip, a deep crease marring the space between her brows. She rubbed at it slowly. 'Can we please talk about this later?'

Gabriella huffed, smoothing down her pastel-pink jumpsuit. 'There is no *later*. If you don't sign it by the end of the week, you'll be lucky if Rafael doesn't recast you altogether. You're making a fool of us both, Sasha.' She peered at her phone as though she weren't in the process of issuing what was clearly a threat. No, Dani didn't understand this world at all. In fact, the urge to stand between the two women was already pressing in on her, and she had to remind herself that her job wasn't to shield Sasha from thinly veiled verbal insults, no matter how badly she wanted to.

'Make sure you lay it on thick with him tonight,' Gabriella continued, finally slipping her phone into her shiny black bag. 'Which reminds me: we need to go shopping!' Another glance Dani's way. 'Will your new chaperone be joining us?'

'I go where she goes.' Dani wanted to remain polite, but her voice was firmer than intended.

'Well, lucky Sasha.' The agent wiggled her brows in a way that might have made some women blush.

In fact, it *did*: Sasha's cheeks turned a rosy pink, made brighter by the white fluorescent office lighting. 'Yes, lucky me,' she muttered, avoiding Dani's amused gaze. And then, quickly, 'Anyway, yes to shopping.'

'Perf! Lunch first? As long as it's a salad, of course.' Gabriella winked. 'Raf will kill me if his beloved Sara Chase isn't in peak condition tomorrow morning.'

'God forbid,' Sasha deadpanned, gathering her bag and following Gabriella into the corridor.

Dani tried not to wrinkle her nose, though the comment lay heavy in her gut. She didn't agree with diets, especially not for aesthetic purposes. Food was supposed to provide joy and nourishment. Sasha had a gorgeous body, but Dani didn't doubt that the industry disagreed. Maybe that was just another reason why she was in such a state of despair.

Have you ever been exhausted? So exhausted that you just want to collapse somewhere and never wake up?

The question still rang in Dani's ears, Sasha's voice echoing hoarse and desperate. Yes, she had felt that exhausted, she'd wanted to say. Constantly after the accident, not something she'd been able to shake off with a few days' rest. But that was completely different. This was Hollywood and, even with the drawbacks, Sasha had everything most people dreamed of.

Did Dani really want to help her throw it all away?

She didn't know if she had a choice. Maybe, she thought as they exited the lobby, it was time to call Marcus.

She could already predict what her boss would say, though: *whatever the client wants, you give to them.*

A new life felt a little extreme, but what else could she do?

Sasha examined herself in the mirror through glazed, vacant eyes. Gabriella had picked out an emerald cocktail dress for her during their shopping trip earlier. Dani had stood blank-faced with her back turned through it all. Uninterested, Sasha would wager—but good at her job. She hadn't let a single fan or paparazzo within a metre of the designer clothing stores, offering one of the smoothest outings Sasha had experienced in years, Gabriella's passive-aggressive remarks about Sasha's 'post-lunch bloating' aside. She capitalised on Sasha being one of the few plus-size actresses in the business, yet still jabbed at her as if she'd rather she fitted the mould. It was exhausting.

To her agent's credit, the dress was a lovely choice, especially for Sasha's curves. The square neckline exposed just enough cleavage and the ruffled hem kissed her lower calves, showcasing the muscles she'd honed for her action role as well as the crystal-embellished Louboutins on her feet. Sasha should have felt beautiful. She certainly looked it. But the woman reflected in the mirror was a stranger, from the fake golden tan to the over-lined lips. She could barely remember what she looked like beneath the thick make-up, all her freckles and imperfections, the things that made her a real person, smoothed over with foundation and powder. Everybody in her life knew only this version of her, the perfect version. Without it, she was nobody to them.

One night, she reminded herself. *One more*

night, and then it'll all be over. It was supposed to be a comfort, but, for the first time, the uncertainty of tomorrow stretched like a vacuum ahead of her. What if she liked herself even less without the mask?

What if she ran away to find that nothing, not even her old self, was waiting for her?

Movement outside the bedroom door had her spine straightening, a knock disturbing the quiet. 'Gabby has instructed me to tell you that the car is here.' Dani's rough voice only scattered Sasha's anxiety further.

'Could you come in a minute?' she called, rearranging her blonde curls over one shoulder with shaky fingers.

Sasha watched Dani stepping warily into the pristine bedroom in the mirror's reflection. She'd dressed for the occasion, though her 'cocktail' attire wasn't much different from her work clothes. Still, something fluttered in Sasha's throat at the sight of the silken black waistcoat with absolutely nothing underneath. The tattoos that had been hidden by sleeves before were revealed, inked on lean, sinewy arms and bare, broad shoulders.

While Sasha's gaze trailed over the black swirls a bird here, a sun there—Dani regarded the space, and Sasha wondered what the bodyguard saw in the sheer, rippling white curtains and plush mattress, the marble floors, to steal so much of her attention. Did she think the lavishness a sign of how spoilt Sasha was? Did she think her absurd to throw it all away?

Sasha told herself it didn't matter, readjusting the straps on her shoulders. 'Please could you fasten the button on my dress?'

'Of course.' Finally, Sasha had earned her attention, and she didn't miss the slight falter in Dani's steps as she raked over Sasha's body. She waited for a compliment, then wondered why. It wasn't Dani's job to tell her she looked nice, or even notice.

'It's Gabriella, by the way.' Sasha's mouth tipped with wry amusement as she turned back to the mirror. If Gabriella heard Dani shorten her name like that, she'd never hear the end of it. *Gabby sounds so tacky,* she'd said when a mutual friend had made the same mistake.

Dani's brows furrowed in the reflection as she fiddled with the small button between Sasha's shoulder blades. When her knuckle, rough and warm, grazed Sasha's skin, Sasha's breath hitched. Being touched by somebody like Dani, sturdy and rugged and unfazed, brought Sasha back into her body. Made her feel a tad more real. Usually, she spent her days floating, being dragged from one responsibility to the next, food and sleep forgotten in the chaos.

'If we won't see her after tonight,' said Dani, 'does it matter?'

Sasha paused. 'You've decided to come with me, then?'

'It's what I'm paid for.' Her tone was as blunt as ever. Sasha envied her detachment, wishing she could make decisions with such cool rationality. Recently, she felt she was nothing but an open wound, and it was getting harder to cover up around the people she worked for.

'But you still don't think I'm doing the right thing,' she commented.

Dani took a step back to lock eyes with Sasha in the mirror. 'What I think doesn't matter, Ms March.'

'Sasha. I hate being called *Ms*.' It was another reminder of her divorce, and, more than that, another barrier between them she didn't need. It would be nice to at least be on friendly terms with the person set to help her get away.

'Okay, Sasha. Do you have any idea of where you want to go?'

She wrung her clammy hands. 'Honestly, no. As long as I get away, I don't care.'

'Can I ask why home isn't an option?'

'LA is full of people who know me—'

Dani lifted a hand. 'I don't mean Hollywood. I mean wherever it is you got that posh accent.'

Sasha didn't like to think about Kent. It had been home once—and far from a posh one—but her parents hadn't been all that supportive during the divorce. She'd gone to the big country house she'd bought for Mum expecting a shoulder to cry on, only to get a million reasons why Sasha should have stayed with Tom, most of them boiling down to maintaining her fame and money. From her first big pay cheque, it was all she'd been good for.

Dad was nowhere to be found; since her parents had separated seven years ago, Sasha heard from him only at Christmas, if that. He had a new family in Brighton with siblings Sasha had never even met. The place where she'd grown up, the place where she'd been most herself, was empty, just like everywhere else.

Of course, she couldn't disclose all of that to a near-stranger. 'Like I said, I'd rather be somewhere nobody knows my name.'

She expected more questions, but Dani only nodded. 'Okay. How about Spain? I happen to know a few places fit for a celebrity. And you can keep your tan topped up.'

Sasha ignored the quip, though the suggestion that she was shallow bothered her, especially coming from Dani. 'Do you think it will be quiet enough?'

'There are quiet places everywhere, if you know where to look.'

Dani seemed so confident as she wandered to the window that Sasha had to ask, 'And how *do* you know where to look?'

'I used to visit family there,' she answered, cast

in the brilliant glow of the dipping sun. Even her silhouette left Sasha tingling, shadows pooling in the hollows of her cheeks and the valleys of her biceps as light rays skimmed over her shoulders. Another tattoo, this time an outline of a star, darkened the back of her ear.

Sasha had been attracted to women before, but never like this. She could observe Dani all day and still want more.

When she didn't reply, Dani glanced at her expectantly, and she tried not to blush at being caught as she joined her at the window.

'Then that's where we'll go.' Sasha's whisper was wobbly. She wasn't sure when they'd got so close, only that Dani's unreadable gaze, the colour of smooth honey in this light, was enough to burn a hole through her. Her bare arms pebbled with goosebumps that she hoped weren't too visible.

And then Dani hopped away when another voice sliced between them. 'Go where?'

Sasha tried to gather her composure before she faced her agent. *Just one more night, and then... Spain.*

On the threshold, Gabriella was all shimmer and smoke, wearing a black floor-length gown cinched at the waist by a corset bodice. Suspicion sparkled with her pearls—clearly, she'd seen them standing closer than had been necessary.

Face heating, Sasha backed away from the window, forcing her mouth into something she hoped resembled a smile. 'I was just telling Dani that there are a few afterparties happening tonight. What do you think: Chantal's or Nick's?'

'Chantal's obviously.' Gabriella rolled her eyes, and Sasha could relax. 'Nick's will only end in sex, drugs and vomit, not necessarily in that order.' She assessed Dani's outfit, likely scrutinising the tattoos, the likes of which Sasha had been banned from getting. *They're so ugly on women,* she'd claimed. Yet nothing about Dani was ugly.

'You look very...nice,' was the best Gabriella could do.

'Thank you, Gabs. I can tell you really mean it.' Dani's biceps flexed as she offered an arm to Sasha. 'Shall we?'

Sasha almost chuckled at the disgust on Gabriella's face. She wasn't used to being out-snarked, especially not by somebody as direct as Dani.

'Gab*riella*,' the agent emphasised. And then, as though attempting to reassert her dominance, she tutted and picked up a tin of bronzer from the vanity, sweeping it across Sasha's cheeks with a fluffy make-up brush. 'I told you we should have hired a make-up artist, darling. This foundation is too pale for your skin.'

Fighting a scowl, Sasha squirmed away to link arms with Dani, more of that heat crackling where their bare skin met. Dani's sturdy presence felt like a shield against Gabriella's barbs, especially when Sasha knew that, come tomorrow, she'd never have to hear them again.

It made her brave enough to shoot out, 'You have lipstick on your teeth.'

She brushed past Gabriella with more strength than she'd felt in a long time. When the corner of Dani's mouth folded with barely stifled amusement, she wondered if perhaps she finally had somebody on her side.

At least she wasn't walking into her last party completely alone.

CHAPTER FOUR

THIS BIG-SHOT DIRECTOR of Sasha's owned the largest yacht in the marina. The white ship, aglow with golden lights across every deck, loomed like a giant over the cruises and sailboats, casting indigo shadows across the moonlit shore.

Show off. Such an extravagant display of wealth made Dani's stomach turn. This guy wanted everyone in Saint-Tropez to know he was stinking rich, and, judging from the audience they received as they pulled up to the harbour, he'd achieved it.

Cameras flashed and crowds marvelled as Dani assisted Sasha out of the car. Tucked away in the back seat, the celebrity looked meek. Her eyes were wide, shoulders hunched, as she regarded the surrounding commotion with apprehension. Anybody watching would see, clearly, that she didn't want to be here. Maybe they had more in common than Dani had thought, because she wasn't all that keen, either. The glamorous parties she ventured into on the job were tolerable, mostly, but this was excess to the highest degree. Anybody with their feet on solid ground could see that.

'You okay?' Dani asked quietly, offering her hand. Gabriella was already out and mingling with whoever complimented her dress the loudest, batting her bouncy locks and posing as though she were one of the A-listers.

Sasha's nod was unconvincing, but her cool palm fell into Dani's with finality as she stepped out. She smoothed the wrinkles from her dress, the jewel tones wrapped around her luscious curves captivating. There was no denying her beauty; it had been enough to give Dani pause in the bedroom earlier. There had been a vulnerability to her in that mirror, perfectly hidden now, that had left Dani seeing her clearly for the first time, even with all the make-up and hairspray-fixed curls. She looked like a movie star, but she didn't move through the world like one.

Perhaps, once, she'd just been a woman like any other. A woman like Dani.

'Where to?' Dani glanced around. She wasn't afraid to admit that she was out of her depth here. Some elegantly clad guests were alighting the cruise at the end of the dock, but a great number socialised on the marina, likely hoping to garner some attention.

She didn't get an answer, though she felt Sasha harden to stone as a dark-haired man with stubble and a smug pout to his lips approached.

'Fashionably late, as always.' His accent was smooth American, eyes icy blue, but Dani was more unsettled by the fact that he wasn't wearing socks with his shoes, tanned, hair-dusted ankles on show between the too-short hem of his navy trousers and the brown loafers on his feet. If bare, sweaty feet were in style now, Dani was glad not to know a lick about it.

The man's piercing gaze fell on Dani, and he looked her up and down as though she were something he'd picked off the floor. 'Is this the new bodyguard I've been hearing so much about?'

Sasha swept her breeze-tousled curls over one shoulder. 'I suppose nothing stays private here, does it?'

'With Gabriella?' He laughed, revealing prominent incisors and pretty-boy dimples. 'Definitely not.'

Ah. So *this* was the ex-husband. Dani examined him more thoroughly, curiosity piqued. It didn't surprise her that he'd cheated, something about his good looks giving the impression of oily rather than pleasant. The type of man who looked at women as if he owned them, who walked into a room ready to take, take, take. Dani had worked with a few in the force, though they'd been far more rugged around the edges.

'Do me a favour, babe.' He leaned closer to Sasha. Dani made to give them privacy, but Sasha's hand remained unrelentingly tight in hers.

An unexpected anger sparked. Was there more here than just a cheating scandal? Was he a threat?

She straightened taller at the thought, ready to step between them if necessary.

His grin didn't waver as he uttered, 'Don't cause a scene tonight. Nobody wants to be reminded of the divorce.'

What an arsehole. Instinctively, Dani stepped forward, the stench of his liquor-laced breath stinging her nostrils. Her show of warning seemed to amuse him rather than offend him.

'I see she's taking her job very seriously,' he mused to Sasha, then patted Dani on the shoulder. 'Simmer down. Good dog.'

Arsehole suddenly felt too kind a word for what he was.

'Be careful, mate,' she growled. 'I'm all bite.'

He whistled through his teeth, the sound dripping in arrogant amusement.

Sasha tugged Dani's bristling body back gently and tipped her head to him in defiance. Dani didn't like it. She'd rather stick between them, where he couldn't touch Sasha.

Still, Sasha held her own, saying, 'If you don't want a scene, Tom, maybe just stay away from me tonight.'

Immediately, Dani saw beyond Tom's facade to something ugly and vengeful beneath: a twist of his upper lip, a flex of his fingers. 'Are you trying to ruin this for both of us? You know Raf wants us playing happy families.'

'I'll give Rafael what he wants, but I don't owe you anything, so back off. *Please.*'

Tom narrowed his eyes and glanced at the cameras surrounding them. He'd gained an audience since the conversation had started.

Then, too quickly for her to stop it, his lips clashed against Sasha's, his tight grip bunching the satin around her hips.

Dani acted on a wave of roiling disgust and gut instinct. She prised Tom away by the shoulder with enough force to send him stumbling. She could barely see through the bright camera flashes and dots of anger flooding her vision.

Both annoyance and shock flared through his nostrils, hand smudging the lipstick on his mouth. 'What the *hell* are you doing?'

'My job,' Dani snapped. 'How about you go and enjoy the party before you embarrass yourself any more than you already have?'

'Sasha, tell your little guard dog that I'm your damn husband.'

'*Ex*-husband,' Sasha spat, voice trembling. Proof enough that Dani had done the right thing. 'Don't ever touch me like that again.'

He sneered at Sasha again, as if Dani didn't exist at all. 'You're pathetic. I'll be glad when Rafael finally realises that,' was all he said as he stumbled towards a group of similarly smarmy men sipping champagne.

Dani gritted her teeth and angled her body over Sasha's in an attempt to conceal her from the crowd. Sasha's eyes were wide, face pale, fingers knotted together at her waist. Dani resisted the urge to unknot them, afraid her nails were about to draw blood.

'Say the word, and I'll take you home,' promised Dani. With this much adrenaline coursing through her, it was an effort to keep her voice gentle. She wasn't usually so quick to anger, but she wanted to smack that smug smirk right off Tom's face.

Sasha blinked the tears from her eyes. Dani couldn't be sure if she'd even heard her, so she ushered her towards the railings of the docks, where the shadows would better hide them.

'Sasha,' she said, hand curling around her arm. There was no use asking if she was okay, because she wasn't, though Dani could see her mask slowly reassembling itself through shallow breaths. A talented actress indeed. 'What do you need?'

With a shudder, Sasha chewed on her bottom lip and sagged against the railing. Now Dani saw it. Too much of it. This wasn't just a woman tired of the hassle that came with fame. This was a woman who was struggling. Suffering. And nobody else in this marina seemed to see it. Nobody had stepped in for her. Nobody had forced Tom away.

'I need this night to be over,' Sasha whispered.

'You don't have to go in there.'

She considered it, dimples pressing into her chin as she worked to control her breathing. 'If I leave now, Gabriella will come after me. I'm her *star.*' The word was filled with derision. 'She needs me on that boat. If I can pretend for one more night like everything's fine, it will give us more time to get out tomorrow.'

'You know, you don't have to sneak away. You can tell them.'

Sasha laughed humourlessly and turned towards the water, the warm breeze fanning her hair. 'It doesn't work like that here.'

As though to prove it, Sasha's name was called again, this time by Gabriella. The agent sauntered over in her tall heels, tutting. 'What on earth are you doing? It's time to board!'

Sasha was dragged away before either of them could protest, Dani trailing them to the dock, where guests were still boarding. A few of them were quick to garnish Sasha with attention, complimenting her dress and asking how the movie was going, but when she answered, they'd already shifted their attention to the next shiny thing.

Suddenly, Dani missed the simplicity of her old career. In the police force, people usually said what they meant. They didn't disguise their bitterness with superficial conversation.

But that life was over and, at least here, Dani had nothing to lose.

She just wished she could say the same about Sasha.

CHAPTER FIVE

GABRIELLA PARADED SASHA across the glossy teak decks, her hand growing increasingly tight around Sasha's wrist as though she sensed that Sasha wanted to—*planned* to—run when given half the chance. Her other hand quivered as she gulped down a flute of bitter champagne, and then another, another, while socialising with strangers who acted like friends, and old friends who acted like strangers. Even without Gabriella's iron grip, there was no escaping them, guests dripping like jewels across every corner of the opulent ship: lounging on pristine white couches under glittering chandeliers; perched on spiral staircases to observe the lower decks; splashing in the mammoth Jacuzzi in chic bikinis. The yacht cut through the glittering sea seamlessly, but Sasha still felt nauseous not half an hour into the charter, and, worse, claustrophobic. At least on land, she could plot a swift exit.

At her back, Dani's presence remained a steady pressure. A comfort, she could admit to herself, especially after the way she'd handled the incident with Tom back at the marina.

I'm all bite. A thrill had jolted through Sasha at that confident uttering, the easy way Dani had pushed his staggering body away. Her strength was addictive, and it wasn't only envy that left Sasha's stomach hot.

When Dani had asked what Sasha needed, Sasha hadn't known the answer. It had been a long, long time since she'd received such a question, if ever, but it had fallen from Dani's tight lips as naturally as gossip currently was from the guests.

'So, you've signed the contract now, yes?' Gabriella tugged Sasha away from the bar, which seemed already to have been drained by Sasha's co-star Jayden. The break-out actor played her trustworthy, tech-savvy best friend in the Sara Chase movie, but off-screen he was vapid and self-absorbed—and drunk.

Sasha glowered when the actor's hand landed on a stewardess's backside, and caught Dani's jaw clench as she noticed, too. As the night wore on, it would only get worse.

Gabriella clicked her fingers in Sasha's face to steal back her attention, and her grip around the stem of her flute tightened enough to endanger the delicate crystal glass.

'Not yet,' she said flatly—but Gabriella had known that before asking.

'Sasha, what are we going to tell Rafael when he asks tonight, hm?'

'We can tell him that it's ten years' worth of terms and conditions and I'm a slow reader.'

'You're pathetic,' Gabriella snapped, a sneer marring her usual beauty.

Pathetic. The same thing Tom had called Sasha earlier, because any show of resistance against their control was surely a flaw on her part.

Sasha averted her gaze to the moonlight-limned horizon, the sea breeze rustling her curls. Tutting, Gabriella smoothed them back, her unnecessarily forceful tug leaving a sting across Sasha's scalp. She bit her tongue. Always biting her tongue.

The urge to look at Dani taunted her again, and she was surprised to find how quickly she was learning to seek her out in the face of discomfort. But Dani couldn't protect Sasha from this. Nobody could. That was why running away was the only answer.

Without permission, Dani's words echoed in her mind over the rippling sound of the waves. *You know, you don't have to sneak away. You can tell them.*

Sasha opened her mouth to say it, right there and then. *I quit. I don't want this. We're done here.*

As always, the words clogged in her throat. What good would it do? She was already in a contract, and she was certain Gabriella would sooner push her overboard than let her walk off this yacht free. To end their partnership, they would both need to agree, in writing, and the agent would never do that. Sasha had seen as much with other clients: long, exhausting battles that only Gabriella won, if not because she kept them chained to her, then because she had publicist friends who were eager to help her drag their names through the mud with all sorts of terrible tabloid headlines upon their departure. Industry friends who would agree never to hire that person again, just because Gabriella asked them not to. Anything to make them regret walking away.

Nobody left her prison and survived, at least not in any way that counted. Even Sasha's lawyer had admitted it would be a struggle to escape her current contracts.

A pinch at her hip had her startling, Gabriella's manicured nails digging into Sasha's flesh. 'Smile,' she commanded. 'Rafael's on his way over.'

Sasha turned away from the railings, head already pounding against the music and overzealous laughter floating from every deck. She caught Dani's eye, only to find an unexpected softness in her expression. She stood a few feet away, poised as though ready for anything. Sasha wondered how it was that nobody else had so much as looked at her tonight. She was the most disarming, magnetic, self-assured person here, and the most natural, bare-faced save for the dark layer of mascara, which revealed a hidden green in her eyes. She gave Sasha an almost imperceptible nod as though to say, *I'm here*.

It gave Sasha the strength to face the director.

Rafael was certainly impossible to ignore, draped in only a black silk kimono and swimming shorts, chiselled torso on display for all to see. At sixty, the director had earned his silver-fox status, but even without his charming smirk and high cheekbones, his good looks, witty personality and alluring spark ensured people flocked to him. He was forever found at the centre of every crowd, moving through the world with an ease that most could only envy.

Sasha had been desperate to impress him from the first moment she'd met him on another set last spring, and it wasn't until filming had begun back in the US a few weeks ago that the sparkle had finally dulled, veil lifted. He'd humiliated her. In front of her peers, her colleagues, her supposed friends. He'd given Tom completely different directions from Sasha, asking him to turn a simple dialogue scene of them bickering into something intimate. Apparently, he'd wanted Sasha's surprise to be *genuine*. Wanted to capture 'raw, unexpected emotion' when Tom kissed her. Any decent director would have warned her beforehand that her ex-husband's tongue was about to enter her mouth, hands about to roam her body, with half a dozen cameras to capture the moment he attempted to lift up her shirt. Not to mention the lack of intimacy co-ordinator on set. In the script, the romance had been subtle, the only saving grace, but Rafael had changed his mind.

And then, when Sasha had recoiled, offering disgust instead of Rafael's anticipated surprise, he'd poked fun. *Oh, dear. I see now why Tommy required a little something on the side during the marriage. Didn't take you for a prude, March.*

She could still hear the snide laughter echoing around the set, still see Tom's eyes glittering with vindication, because his narrative had been confirmed: it had been Sasha who wasn't enough, not him. Surely, she must have deserved an unfaithful husband.

Rafael held his arms out now with a warmth Sasha no longer trusted, spilling his champagne in the process. 'There she is. My superstar.' His brown eyes scraped up and down Sasha's figure. 'Ravishing, darling. That husband of yours was just telling me how stunning you looked, and I had to see for myself.'

She tamped down the urge to remind Rafael that Tom was certainly *not* anything of hers, knowing it would only be in vain. Once the movie was wrapped up and marketing began, Rafael wanted to tell the world how his movie had brought two broken hearts back together, rekindling the Hollywood romance everyone, supposedly, was rooting for.

'You're too kind, Raf,' she said instead. And then, when Gabriella nudged her: 'Of course, it was Gabriella who picked out the dress. I'd be useless without her.'

'Of course,' he agreed, not without a sultry smirk towards her agent. But it was still Sasha's hair he twirled around his finger as he got closer. Close enough for her to smell the sharp liquor on his breath. She heard a shuffle behind her, Dani's proximity sending a lightning bolt through her spine. 'So, March, when are you going to put me out of my misery, hm? We can't have a Sara Chase franchise without Sara Chase.'

'You'll have the signatures by tomorrow noon,' Gabriella promised before Sasha could so much as let out an 'erm' of consideration.

'Why not tonight?' His hand snaked around her waist, and she fought not to squirm. 'Must you always make us men wait?'

'It's a lot to consider.'

He narrowed his eyes. 'Is it?' He plucked another flute from a passing waiter and shoved it into Sasha's hands. 'Here, have a few more of these and then get back to me.'

Gabriella laughed. Sasha didn't, until the point of Gabriella's stiletto dug into her big toe. She sipped, obedience the only way to get through the interaction. A frosty sensation across her skin alerted her to Tom's heavy scrutiny. He leaned lazily against the bar behind with Jayden and a pretty woman she didn't know, eyes hooded and movements swaying as if they were sailing through far choppier seas.

She hated him. It wasn't a new realisation, but it sliced through her all the same as he blew her a kiss and then nuzzled into the woman's neck with new determination. If he thought it made her jealous, it made him the fool. She knew too much of him now to ever envy the object of his affection.

Thankfully, Rafael was soon distracted by a tall, attractive man who spoke with a thick French accent. She let out a breath, turning back to the water and squeezing her eyes closed as her empty stomach began to churn.

Gabriella sidled close, leaving a violent hiss in Sasha's ear before she departed, too. 'Whatever game you're playing will only end with one loser. Sort your shit out. Now.'

She tried not to let the threat touch her, gripping the yacht's railing fiercely as all the champagne she'd downed threatened to make a reappearance.

It didn't matter. She'd be out of here come tomorrow.

But she still wondered if it would be enough. To what lengths would Gabriella go to ensure she won? Right now, with her throat searing and the world so loud around her, it was hard for Sasha to imagine a future where she'd be free. Hard to imagine a life that wasn't filled with all this dread.

And then her pinkie finger prickled, a zap of energy crawling up her arm, and she opened her eyes to see Dani's hand beside hers on the railing. She still faced the party, and didn't look at Sasha at all even when Sasha's head rose in surprise, but she was there. Comforting her.

Something tugged at Sasha: the urge to close the gap between them, bury herself in this new, unexpected safety.

Dani's finger twitched against hers, just once, and then she pulled away, and Sasha remembered that she wasn't a friend, and she certainly wasn't a soft place to land. She was here because Sasha paid her to be here, and, really, that meant she was the same as everyone else.

Except she didn't *feel* like everyone else as Sasha continued to endure the night's socialising. The opposite. If the lines blurred, it was because Sasha needed them to. She needed someone she could trust, and Dani Sharpe was the closest thing to it.

When the silhouette of the Saint-Tropez coastline returned to view, Sasha could finally breathe. She'd made it through the night, and she'd never have to see these people again. As they docked, a cluster of photographers still waited, likely hoping for shots of drunk celebrities and influencers. They had plenty to go at: Sasha could see Rafael and his Frenchman reenacting *Titanic* for the marina's captive audience. She began shuffling towards the back of the boat, hoping to make a swift exit. Gabriella was giving her the silent treatment, which meant she had no reason to linger. Every so often, Dani's touch fluttered at the small of Sasha's back as she tried to avoid intoxicated guests, keeping her upright when sharp elbows and heavy shoulders barged past her to get in their last drinks. They'd probably be here until morning.

As she reached the deckhand assisting guests off the boat, Tom stumbled on her heels, slurring her name. This close to the marina, when she'd nearly escaped, she didn't deign to look back at him. Relief replaced her apprehension as she lifted her foot to alight, finally taking her first step away from everything that made her unhappy—

Only for Tom's weight to shove her sideways, right as she reached the low dock.

Sasha toppled, grasping for something to clutch onto, but the world swam in front of her too quickly for her to halt. She was falling, the lapping waves beneath rising to meet her.

And then the cold darkness chewed her up.

CHAPTER SIX

DANI SHOVED PAST that bumbling arse of an ex as soon as she saw Sasha toppling, but when she reached out, she grasped only the night's balmy air. The sound of the splash ricocheted through her, her muscles taut as she readied herself to follow. Her stomach lurched, fighting that instinct. She hadn't been in the water since Eve, and her breath felt sharp as a blade when she looked at the black depths below.

But there was no other option. No time. Sasha needed her.

She'd expected that her adrenaline would have been sluggish to wake after so long left dormant, but it pulsed through her as though it had been waiting impatiently beneath her skin. As the gasping guests and flashing lights peeled away, Dani surrendered to it without question.

She kicked off her shoes and jumped in.

The water submerged her completely, in more ways than by just its chill, her vision blackening around the edges as the ghost of Eve's final scream pierced her ears. For a moment, she was back there, choking on mucky river water while icy fingers slipped away and then disappeared altogether. She gasped for breath, realising that even as she battled with a current that didn't exist here, her body was doing what it was supposed to: reaching for the flailing limbs beneath the water.

She found Sasha's waist and gripped her tightly enough that the memories receded. Sasha resurfaced with a violent cough, hair plastered to her face and mascara running down her cheeks. Fear and shock pierced through her features as her fist curled into Dani's waistcoat.

'It's okay. I've got you,' Dani breathed, reassuring herself as much as she was Sasha. 'I've got you.'

Clarity sharpened Sasha's features as she caught her breath, steadying against the languid caress of the waves. Against Dani. She craned her neck and sent out a glare to Tom and the surrounding guests, made all the more merciless by the night's harsh shadows. 'Arsehole!' she bellowed, voice hoarse.

Still, Dani saw the wobble of her chin and knew the mask was dangling by a thread.

'I didn't mean to, babe. I swear!' Tom replied. Two deckhands flanked him to stop him staggering after her. Under the golden fairy lights, the corner of his mouth lifted, and he hid his amusement behind the back of his hand. 'You have to admit, this is damn funny.'

Disgust left Dani snarling. It took every bit of self-restraint to stop herself saying something she'd regret, something that would leave her without a job if it got back to Marcus. The deckhand squatted to offer them both a hand, but Sasha reared back with just as much vehemence, turning away from the yacht. 'I'm not going anywhere near him or that yacht again.'

With Sasha's teeth chattering, it was all Dani could do to guide her back to shore herself. 'Come on. Let's get you home.'

They paddled quickly, aware that every second spent here was another photograph that would soon litter social media and magazines. It wasn't only paparazzi that stood around, scrambling to get closer, but onlookers with their phones out, recording Sasha's humiliation without an ounce of shame. In the light of their torches, her cheeks blazed red, and as they finally reached the pebbled shore, Dani did everything she could to shield Sasha, including mutter, 'Your dress,' when she glimpsed a slither of black lace underwear beneath the bunched silk.

Sasha swore, peeling her hem down quickly. She'd also lost her shoes in the water, both of them barefoot and sopping.

'You're not hurt?' Dani checked her over. Her body hadn't yet realised that the threat had passed, worry still pounding in time with her accelerated heartbeat.

Sasha shook her head. 'I just want to go. Please, just get me out of here.'

The rawness in her voice scraped right through Dani. She'd been wrong, before, about everything she'd thought Sasha March was, everything she'd endured. No amount of fame and money in the world could heal the wounds inflicted on her by the people on that yacht. No wonder she wanted to disappear.

And it would only be worse tomorrow, when the pictures were published. If not for Sasha's plans to run away, she would have to get up, go to work with the people who had watched this happen. *Allowed* it to happen.

Dani tugged her close as they walked up the beach together, demanding a jacket from the first face she saw, a tall man wearing a blazer as if he'd hoped to disguise his way on board. He floundered until Dani shot him a stony glare, and then was quick to empty his pockets and shuck the jacket off. Dani draped it around Sasha's shoulders, and Sasha used it to cover her face as they dived further into the crowd.

A million questions were hurled in her direction.

'Sasha, can you tell us what happened on the yacht?'

'Did Tom push you overboard?'

A foul taste filled Dani's mouth. They barked at Sasha as though they were owed something, and when they didn't get what they wanted, they only began to inch closer, their prods becoming more forceful. Dani's toe smarted when somebody stepped on it with heavy soles.

'Sasha, was this payback for the affair?'

'Is it true you two are fighting constantly on set?'

Dani shoved them back with barely restrained anger. It was an effort not to give into her instincts, an overwhelming effort to keep her breathing even and her tone authoritative, but she did—for the woman at her back, who gripped onto her waistcoat like a lifeline.

Finally, they reached one of the many sleek black cars parked in wait, and Dani ushered Sasha into the back seat, glad to finally have her safe from the chaos. On the other side, with her hand gripping the passenger door handle, she hesitated. Usually, she would ride in the front, keeping an invisible wall between herself and the client.

But it didn't feel right to let Sasha sit alone after what she'd faced.

She continued to the back, not even a little bit sorry when she opened the door so quickly that it thwacked into the gut of a particularly relentless paparazzo. Her damp clothes squeaked against the leather seats as she slid inside, slamming the door closed behind her. She uttered the address of Sasha's villa to the driver, who eyed them in the rear-view but said nothing.

Now, finally, Dani could focus all of her attention on the hunched woman beside her. She chewed on her bottom lip, wishing there were something she could do to chase away that flat dejection tugging across Sasha's expression. Her gaze was vacant as she watched the coast disappear behind them, arms locked tightly around her middle.

'You said there wasn't a threat to your safety,' Dani pointed out quietly.

'When Tom's drunk, he's a threat to everyone's safety.'

'I didn't just mean that.' The harassment, the kisses she hadn't wanted, the extra-tight grip of Gabriella's hands. She'd told Dani that the fans were the problem, that coffee in her face was the worst of it, but there hadn't been a soul on that yacht who had cared for Sasha's boundaries and personal space, let alone whether she got hurt or not.

Sasha turned to her finally, lashes damp from more than just their splash. 'Thank you for getting me out.'

'It's my job,' Dani said, perhaps because she needed the reminder, too. The claustrophobic crowd hadn't fazed her, not really, but she could still feel the salt drying on her skin like grit as the weight of diving into the water finally hit her. The last time she'd felt like this, damp, cold and reeling with excess adrenaline, she'd watched Eve disappear. Even now, she could feel the marshy riverbanks under her buckled knees, taste the bitter silt after she'd screamed so hard that the water had poured into her mouth.

She looked down at her hands to find them shaking.

When she saw Sasha watching, she clenched her fists and hid them between her thighs quickly, realising she hadn't yet put on her seat belt—and neither had Sasha.

Carefully, because she didn't want to intrude on Sasha's space as everybody else had all night, Dani reached over her to tug the seat belt across her torso. She heard the hitch of Sasha's breath as their faces landed inches away, the smell of diluted perfume and sickly-sweet champagne mingling between them. Without warning, the car jolted over an unexpected bump, and Dani's arm fell onto the headrest beside Sasha as she worked to keep upright.

The air tasted thick and foreign, all memories of that dark day gone, and she almost forgot what she'd intended to do. Why Sasha was suddenly inches away, all wide, glistening eyes and mascara-freckled cheeks, red lipstick dried into the indents of her plump bottom lip.

'Sorry.' She was. She truly hadn't meant to get this close, not after everything.

'It's okay.' Sasha's clumsy fingers grazed Dani's as she took over, clicking the belt into place.

With an uncomfortable clearing of her throat,

Dani sat back and fastened herself in. There was a new ache behind her ribs, a need for Sasha to know that Dani intended to set things right. She hadn't realised before now, the lengths she was willing to go to to make sure her clients felt safe, mostly because she'd never had reason to.

Because nobody else she'd worked for had struggled like this.

The car stopped outside Sasha's gates, driver getting out to open them. Beyond the wrought iron, Sasha's villa resembled a manor house, delicate white balcony and pillars made brighter by the peach walls and outdoor lanterns. Tall stone pines curved over the roof like umbrellas, the green canopy and twisting branches casting dappled moonlight across the blooming garden out front. When Dani had first seen it earlier, she'd wondered why anybody would possibly want to leave such a place. Now, she was as eager to get out of Saint-Tropez as Sasha.

'I don't want to wait until tomorrow,' Sasha said, focus locked on the window again. 'I want to go now.'

'Are you sure? You could do with some rest—'

'I'm sure. God, how could I not be sure?'

Dani felt the desperation in her voice like a string tightening around her.

'All right. Whatever you need,' she replied softly.

After tonight, she wouldn't force Sasha to stay here for a moment longer than necessary.

CHAPTER SEVEN

THEY'D CROSSED THE Spanish border by dawn the next morning. Sasha rubbed the sleep from her eyes as she straightened in the passenger seat, her backside beginning to ache from so many hours sitting. She'd barely dried herself off back at the villa before throwing on her comfiest clothes and packing one meagre bag, ready to leave Saint-Tropez and her old life behind. In the end, she hadn't wanted to hold onto much. Everything in her life was disposable; she'd spent her entire adult life in the limelight, and she had nothing but designer clothes and high-end make-up to show for it.

The idea that she would eventually have to get out of this car, with or without those things, was daunting. Dani was a silent driver: they hadn't spoken in hours, yet every flick of the indicator and quiet hum as she fought back a yawn made Sasha feel less lonely than she had in years. She couldn't remember having company she didn't feel pressure to entertain. Company that just *was*, without expectation. It might have been part of Dani's job to blend in with her surroundings, but she made it seem effortless. In this pocket of the universe, she was all Sasha had, and already it made her world feel smaller. More manageable.

Calm.

Until her phone began to ping with the return of signal. She'd hoped it would have died by now—that way she wouldn't be tempted to use it. She'd considered leaving it in the villa with everything else, but…something had stopped her. It was the final thread tying her to everything familiar, and perhaps she needed time to cut it.

Or maybe not. She wasn't surprised when social media notifications rolled in about last night, but her stomach still began to churn. Comments like, OMG, that's embarrassing! and texts from supposed friends that read, at least you were wearing hot underwear! proved it hadn't even taken a night for the photos to leak. She didn't want to see them, nor did she ever want to talk to most of these people again. Not a single one, not even those she'd considered friends, had asked if she was okay, and that realisation dragged the searing hurt back tenfold. There wasn't a soul out there who cared about her well-being.

So, she wiped her phone, rolled down the window, and threw it in the green shrubbery whizzing by outside. She'd get a new one once they settled.

Dani's brows lifted as she cast Sasha a sidelong glance. Her hair had dried wavier and more tousled than it had been yesterday, curling at the ends where the wind tugged at it, and Sasha couldn't deny that it only made her look more attractive. She'd got so used to perfection that Dani's casual ease made her feel electric. Sasha didn't know what she would have done without her last night. She hadn't wanted to crumple that way, but Dani had let her with those quiet invitations of touch and gentle reassurances.

I've got you. And she had, staving off the crowd with dogged, unquestionable strength. It was the first time Sasha had ever been protected, an addictive feeling, not only because she'd finally felt safe, but because Dani's gravelly demands and tight grip had lit a fire in her.

'That bad?' was all Dani asked, resting her elbow on the open window as her focus returned to the quiet motorway. Her inner arm was a ripple of muscle and ink, difficult to tear away from.

'I didn't look.' Sasha fiddled with the strings of her hoodie. 'The previews were enough.'

'Won't people be worried about you? There must be someone who'll try to report you missing. I'm not saying these people deserve answers, but the media storm will only get worse if they think you're in trouble.'

'I already texted my mum to tell her I'm going on an extended holiday—not that she would've noticed either way. And I left a note back at the villa. My lawyer will handle the rest.' She didn't want anybody to turn this into something that it wasn't. It had been a hurried, flat message in shaky handwriting, written on a napkin and left on the coffee table, where Gabriella would likely lay down her iced oat milk latte in a few hours' time.

Don't look for me. I don't want to be found.

If Gabriella made her the villain for leaving without explanation, then that was okay. As long as she left her alone. As long as Sasha could finally disappear for long enough to get out of her contracts.

Dani shook her head, and Sasha frowned. 'What? You still think I'm doing the wrong thing?'

'No, I think, after what I saw last night, you're more than entitled to be free of it all. I just have a hard time believing that there isn't one person who won't miss you.'

'Well, believe it.' Sasha's tone dripped with bitterness, a lump forming in her throat. She'd thought, at first, that they *did* care. Gabriella had believed in her enough to grant her stardom, after all, and Tom had worked for her affection as if she were all he'd wanted. She'd had friends who had celebrated her successes, been the bridesmaids at her wedding—one who had shared her husband, behind her back, while the others pretended not to know.

After such a painful betrayal, she'd wondered if she was the problem. If everybody treated her as though she was unlovable, didn't that make it true? She'd never had many close friends pre-fame, always on the outskirts: another reason she'd allowed herself to be swept away. For a while, she'd believed that Gabriella had made her beautiful, desirable, talented, *worthy.* She'd never expected that loneliness could follow her across an ocean.

But faced with the divorce, she'd had the time to watch other talents pass through the spotlight. Occasionally they stuck around, but more often than not they faded out quickly. An industry like hers didn't foster kindness or connection, at least not in the circles Gabriella had dragged her into. She'd seen the truth of it, the brutality, too late.

'All they'll miss is the money,' she decided. 'What about you? What's your story, Dani Sharpe?'

'Thought you read all about it in my file,' Dani commented dryly.

'It wasn't very detailed. I assume you don't have a spouse and kids, since you're willing to spend months on end with self-absorbed clients like me.'

Her mouth twitched. 'You'd assume right.'

'And the family you used to visit in Spain?'

'Not very close to them any more.' The nonchalance in Dani's voice wavered, betraying her.

Sasha waited for more, realising that she found

comfort in the cadence of Dani's voice—providing she actually said more than a few words at a time, which hadn't happened very often so far.

'And what about the police?' Sasha prodded when the *more* didn't come. 'Why aren't you still with them?'

Dani didn't respond, though her knuckles whitened over the steering wheel. A step too far. Curiosity niggled in Sasha, but she did her best to quell it. If Dani was willing to put her life on pause for her, she at least deserved privacy.

When Sasha thought about how long that pause might be, the silence suddenly felt too stifling to bear. How long could she truly hide away before needing something to keep her afloat again? What would she even do with so much time to herself? An aimless hermit, no longer having to endure burnout caused by raucous parties and sixteen-hour workdays—how would she survive that level of solitude?

To block out the fear, she turned on the radio, flicking through talk stations and white noise until she came to a pop song she recognised. They remained like that for a while, Sasha falling into a trance as she admired the gorgeous hilly landscapes and tried to forget the rest.

A repulsed scoff fell from her when the first stiff cords of her latest single began to play, finger quick to jab the off button.

'What was that?' Dani asked.

Sasha clenched her jaw. It felt embarrassing to admit that the song was hers, mostly because it wasn't. After the success of her first album, she'd dreamed of songwriting in the studio with renowned artists. Instead, the songs had been written for her, the label claiming they knew exactly how to position her for a number one single. She couldn't remember when she'd stopped trying to argue with them about the childish lyrics and uncharacteristically upbeat melodies. It had been made clear that the alternative was no music career at all. Sasha's stripped-back ballads alone wouldn't be enough to bring in the money. *She* wouldn't be enough. So they'd moulded her into something else, and she'd let them, believing for a while that it made her worth something.

Dani narrowed her eyes and turned the radio back on. Sasha winced at the sound of her voice, made high-pitched and wispy by overproduction.

'Is that...*you*?'

'Believe me, I know it's bad.' She jabbed the radio off again before her ears began to bleed. Of all the things she'd lost over the last few years, it was this that brought her the most shame. A career in music was all she'd ever wanted, but she'd lost her voice. Or, rather, they had stolen it.

'I wouldn't know. My music knowledge expired fifteen years ago.' That same curiosity Sasha had felt not too long ago glimmered in

Dani's eyes. 'What's wrong with it? Are you sick of singing it?'

'No. I never liked it. I used to make music that meant something, at least to me. But the record label wanted something that would sell, and, apparently, that isn't the same thing. So I started singing whatever crap they wrote for me and hoped it would get me enough success that, eventually, I'd be trusted to create for myself again.'

Lines formed on Dani's forehead, and Sasha ached to know what she was thinking. That Sasha was pathetic? That she deserved better? That nobody really cared what sort of songs she sang, because it was all superficial, soulless crap?

No. What Dani said was, 'I'm sorry you lost something you loved.' She tapped her thumb restlessly against the steering wheel. 'I'm sure you could get it back, now you're away from it all.'

Sasha was taken aback by her show of empathy. By how it felt to be heard. *Seen.*

'What?' Dani asked when she could only stare, frozen.

She probably looked like a fool. She gulped down the emotion threatening to spill from her, shaking herself free. 'Nothing. Just…maybe you're right. I hadn't thought that far ahead.'

There was no reason why she couldn't rediscover her love of songwriting again. She'd have all the time in the world—and all the space, with what she'd seen after viewing pictures of the Spanish villa booked under Dani's name last night.

Dani succumbed to her first yawn as the orange light of the morning sun illuminated her face. She'd been driving all night, and they still had hours to go.

'We should stop at the next decent hotel we find,' Sasha decided.

'You sure? We only have…' Dani glanced at her satnav and grimaced '…four and a half hours left.'

Sasha smiled gently, fighting the urge to dam the stray tear rolling down Dani's high cheekbone after another fierce yawn. Yes, she was sure.

Besides, she needed to purchase a few things before they reached their new accommodation. She didn't plan on looking like Sasha March when she began her new life.

CHAPTER EIGHT

'NOT UP TO your usual five-star-hotel standards?' Dani clamped down her smirk as she watched Sasha drink in the tiny B & B room they'd rented. Even in her casual clothes, a smudge of last night's tear-stained make-up darkening her eyes, she stood out like a sore—or, rather, manicured—thumb among the cosy, rustic furniture. In a tiny village outside Girona, nobody would ever think to find the celebrity here.

'It's, er, fine,' Sasha said, and then tripped over the protruding leg of the coffee table. 'Very… snug.'

To be fair, Dani wasn't much happier with the accommodation, mainly because the host, an elderly Spanish lady who had been eager to feed them delicious home-made tortillas for breakfast, had only one room left, and the bed, piled high with pillows, didn't look nearly big enough for them both.

She plopped down on the armchair instead, not before stretching out her stiff limbs. Dani could manage a nap just about anywhere. She kicked out her legs, eyelids already heavy.

'Take the bed,' Sasha said.

'I'm good here, thanks.'

'I slept in the car,' she insisted. 'You need it more.'

'Honestly, I'm fine.'

Without warning, Sasha huffed and attempted to pull Dani out of the armchair with unexpected strength. Not enough to move her, mind, Dani's body already sunk deep into the citrus-patterned cushions. When Sasha's mouth pursed in an endearing pout, Dani laughed, the hoarse sound surprising even her—she couldn't remember the last time she'd heard it.

'Seriously, March?'

Sasha seemed to see the question as a challenge, eyes flaring as she pulled again, this time managing to drag Dani a little further. 'I am capable, you know. I had to do a lot of weight training to play an FBI agent.'

'I believe it.' While her curves were all softness, her biceps and thighs were taut with impressive muscle. Dani realised she was staring a little too intensely and quickly slumped back into the chair. 'I think I'm stronger, unfortunately.'

'Aren't you supposed to do what I say?'

'I'm supposed to sacrifice my comfort to prioritise yours, actually.' But since her shoulder was about to come out of its socket, and since Sasha's sea-salt scent was washing all over her a distracting amount, she rose on achy legs.

A mistake. It left her inches from Sasha, the blonde's forehead level with Dani's chin so she had to look down to really see her. When Sasha breathed, her chest brushed Dani's, and she stilled as though she'd forgotten all about her armchair mission. So did Dani, Sasha's choppy fringe fluttering against her sharp exhale.

Why did Sasha look so off kilter when they were alone? She'd seen it yesterday, too, the way she'd responded to every word and movement Dani made as though…

She didn't know. As though Sasha felt her presence more viscerally than most, maybe. Dani was used to blending into the background, but Sasha seemed to pluck her to the forefront of her attention. Dani had chalked it up to nerves. But it was just the two of them now, and Sasha had to know she could trust her, so why was there still so much uncertainty humming between them?

Was it uncertainty, or something else entirely?

Dani wouldn't let herself entertain that thought. She pulled her arm from Sasha's hand, putting distance between them.

'The armchair is fine.'

'You know, we could just share the bed,' Sasha proposed.

'No, we couldn't.' Dani's tone was sterner than intended, leaving no room for argument. Sasha was young and, after what she'd been through, vulnerable. Dani wouldn't let the lines blur. She'd made that mistake before, and it had ended in heartache. With Eve, she would always wonder if their romantic relationship had contributed to her death. If Dani had been her superior, nothing more, would Eve have heeded her warnings in the river before it had dragged her away?

Pull back, Eve. Now!

The only way to keep people safe was to remain in control. Detached. She couldn't do that if she lay beside her client.

'Fine. Be stubborn.' Sasha huffed and sprawled out on the bed, arms folded over her stomach as she stared up at the ceiling with a shimmer of hurt in her eyes. Proof that Dani had made the right call. She wouldn't be mistaken as a cure for Sasha's loneliness.

Still, in the armchair, Dani watched her for longer than necessary, tracking the flutters of her lids as sleep tugged her down. Only when they closed completely did Dani allow herself to drift off, too.

Dani woke with a start, face crinkling against the low sun bleeding in through the window. She'd been dreaming about the water again, and could still feel the strain as her lungs had filled, every shout pouring more of the river into her mouth. And *her* name echoing in her ears: *Eve, Eve, Eve.*

'Are you okay?' Sasha's voice, frayed with concern, anchored Dani back to the present. She'd forgotten, for a moment, where she was, but now the B & B room rearranged itself in a blur of colour as she sat up in the armchair. Had she been shouting? Had Sasha heard?

That worry was quickly swept away by another pressing thought as she took in the contents strewn across the bed. Hair dye, scissors and a striped towel poured out from a paper bag that had certainly not been there before.

'Have you been out without me?' Her voice was sharp with accusation as she hopped out of the armchair.

'I got restless. I didn't mean to wake you.' Oblivious to the way Dani bristled, Sasha opened the box of dye and scanned the instruction leaflet.

'Are you seriously that *dim*?' It came out harsher than expected, but there was no time or energy for filters. 'You hired me to keep you safe, and then you go out on your own after running away from your own life not twenty-four hours ago?'

The leaflet fell to Sasha's side. 'I was fine. It's a small village, and the shop's only around the corner.'

'Jesus Christ.' If Sasha was going to go swanning off whenever she wanted, what was the point of Dani being here at all?

'You needed the rest, and I needed this.' She shook the box of dye forcefully.

Dani let out a disbelieving scoff. 'What, to touch up your roots? I understand, to people like you, that's life or death, but did you even *think* what might happen if you were spotted? *You're* the one who wanted to disappear—'

'And I will!' Sasha turned the box around, displaying a model with glossy brunette hair.

All right, maybe that made a little more sense. Sasha would be less recognisable without her signature blonde waves. Still, the tension in Dani's body didn't ease. 'Don't do that again. At least not until things settle. I can't protect you if I don't know where you are.'

'I'll take that as an apology.' Sasha attempted lightness, but Dani was in no mood for it.

'Take it as an order.' She pinched the box to inspect the colour more closely. '*Iced-coffee brown.* Not very glam, is it?'

Sasha snatched it back. 'And what exotic shade do you use? Cherry red?'

'Garnet, actually, which at least isn't named after a beverage.'

'Is this funny to you?'

'Am I laughing?' Maybe Dani was taking it too far, especially with the glower she wore, but she needed to know that Sasha wasn't a complete wildcard. She needed to know she would remain close. *Safe.*

But Sasha only matched her ire, jutting her chin in defiance. 'No. I think that would take a miracle.'

'Whereas you're an absolute riot, aren't you?'

Her eyes narrowed to slits at that, and she looked at the scissors as though she were contemplating using them as a weapon. Dani would have liked to see her try, especially in her current sour mood. She was still on red alert after her dream, still somewhere else, fighting to stay above water.

'Are you going to chop it all off as well?' she questioned.

Sasha raked her hand through her hair, inspecting the ends. 'Maybe. I haven't decided.'

Dani scrutinised her. She kept expecting Sasha to change her mind, turn back. Even if the people she surrounded herself with, worked for, were obnoxious, dangerous arseholes, it took a lot of strength to walk away from everything that was familiar. Dani would know. This, as superficial as it was, felt like the final, determining step.

She perched on the bed and peered into the shopping bag to find a colourful assortment of crisps, biscuits, and sweets. 'Nutritional.'

'I haven't been allowed to eat so much as a Pringle for the last five months. You'll forgive me if I want to enjoy a few snacks,' Sasha snapped, and then marched off into the bathroom.

A seed of guilt planted itself in Dani's stomach.

She hadn't meant it like that. Certainly hadn't wanted to sound like that toxic, diet-obsessed agent of hers.

The room fell into silence as Sasha lathered dye into her hair in front of the mirror, the door left open as if she wanted Dani to watch—so of course Dani didn't. She busied herself on her laptop for a while, researching the villa property once more to plan the security measures she'd take, and the ones that were already there. Sasha had been the one to choose it, a vacation rental that few people outside the more affluent regions of Spain could afford. It was perched on a hill overlooking the coast, flanked by beaches and fishing villages.

The photographed landscape summoned fond, sun-soaked memories of Dani's childhood. Her dad's side of the family lived in Marbella, and he'd spent many summers teaching her to swim while Aunt Irene and her mother watched from the sand. She wasn't naive enough to think she would enjoy herself half as much this time around, but the twinge of nostalgia was the first vaguely pleasant feeling she'd had in a while—if not also an uncomfortable reminder of how far she'd drifted from her family.

She'd never been great at keeping in touch anyway, but isolating herself from anyone who knew about her grief had been intentional. Not just for Eve, either. Her father had died five years ago;

there would never be another holiday with him, and the thought of visiting Aunt Irene without him there to fill the awkward silences only made her feel empty. She wasn't sure she'd be welcome after so long spent avoiding text messages and phone calls.

Still, Spain had once been Dani's second home, and she hoped perhaps Sasha might find a similar sense of belonging.

She deserved that, at least.

CHAPTER NINE

SASHA TRIED TO recognise herself in the mirror. She'd thought that if she dyed her hair to something close to its natural colour, she might feel more like the person she'd been before. Not Sasha March. Sasha Jane Marten, a normal woman from a normal town.

Instead, she felt like someone new. A stranger. She didn't know if it was worse or better. Shakily, she picked up the scissors she'd borrowed from the B & B owner and grabbed a fistful of damp hair. Maybe this wasn't a good idea. The last time she'd attempted an at-home haircut was at the age of fifteen, and it had ended with a disastrously choppy fringe and a lopsided bob.

She sighed and opened the bathroom door to find Dani scrolling on her phone with her legs stretched out on the bed. Sasha would have liked to take in the sight of her this relaxed, but Dani had already shifted at the sound of the creaking hinge. A muscle in her jaw feathered as she took in Sasha's bare legs and shoulders, and Sasha clutched the soft bath towel a little tighter to her full chest. She told herself that she was glad when it was the only reaction she got, but, honestly, she wouldn't have minded Dani taking a few extra seconds to drink her in. Maybe that made her superficial, as Dani had implied her to be, or maybe it was just that she liked the way Dani looked at her. *Saw* her, not the masks she tried to wear.

'How handy are you with a pair of scissors?' Sasha pushed aside her pride to ask.

Dani locked her phone and placed it down. 'Lucky for you, I spent my childhood in a salon. My mum's a hairdresser.' She moved off the bed and pointed at the buzzed side of her head. 'You can imagine her devastation when I came home with this.'

Sasha handed her the scissors as she approached. 'You said you weren't close to your family.'

'We don't really talk any more.' In the cramped bathroom, still sticky from the hot-shower steam, Dani kicked the wastebasket closer to the sink, then motioned for Sasha to sit. The only available surface was the edge of the bathtub, so she dipped her toes into the foamy bubbles left behind from her pomegranate shower gel and picked at the fluff of her towel.

'How short are we going?' Dani asked.

'I don't know. Shoulder length, maybe?'

Sasha fought a shudder as Dani began combing through her hair, gentler than expected as she teased out the knots at the base of her shoulder blades.

'I can't promise it'll be anything glamorous. It's been a while since I've cut anyone's hair but my own.'

'I trust you. Sort of.'

A snort, and then the sound of the scissors snipping filtered through the quiet. Sasha licked her chapped lips, an unexpected relief whooshing from her as the first waves fell off her back.

Dani paused. 'Don't tell me you've changed your mind.'

'No. No, the opposite.' Sasha fought back tears. 'I wanted to cut my hair years ago, but Gabriella wouldn't let me.'

'Did you ever consider doing it anyway?'

'I tested the waters by having my stylist cut off a few inches. Gabriella fired her immediately, then didn't put me forward for any auditions until it grew back.'

Dani paused. 'She...*punished* you?'

'My hair wasn't mine any more. Nothing was mine any more. She wanted to make sure I knew that.'

'Weirdly enough, she sounds like my mum.' Dani began cutting less tentatively now, and Sasha saw her frown sharpen with focus in the foggy reflection of the marbled tiles.

Sasha's heart thudded against the towel. This shouldn't have felt so intimate, but every brush of knuckles against her damp skin left her electrified.

'Dani…'

'Hm?'

'When you were asleep, you said something.' She knew she was treading dangerous waters, but she couldn't quell the ache to know more of the woman who had, in less than a day, become her anchor.

She felt Dani's grip on her hair waver. Like in the car, she gave no response.

'You said "Eve".'

Still nothing. Sasha dipped her chin. It felt as though it were only her with her chest open, problems laid bare. It was her own fault for expecting something more. For *wanting* more.

Dani leaned closer as she worked on the front of Sasha's hair, feathering the angled scissors with far more expertise than she'd let on. Now, Sasha was eye level with her toned stomach, the hem of her T-shirt riding above her waistband to display a pale stretch of skin. Sasha wasn't sure whether she wanted to move away or pull Dani closer. She knew what she *should* want, but her heart pounded too loudly to listen to her head.

She moved her gaze to her tightly clenched fists as heat began to rise up her neck. Hair landed on her shoulder, and as Dani brushed it off, a fire licked over the curve of her collarbone, Dani's touch far more delicate than necessary.

It was this that gave Sasha the confidence to raise her head once more, her eyes trailing over Dani's stomach and the slight curve of her breasts to meet her gaze.

This time, it was Dani's turn to falter: proof that Sasha wasn't imagining the cloud between them, thick as the humid hours before a thunderstorm.

'You should add great conversationalist to your Stars profile,' she said flatly. A challenge, because at least when they were making quips at one another, Dani was talking to her. Sarcasm was fast becoming their language, and, as frustrating as it was not being able to penetrate Dani's steel, Sasha would take it over the artificial small talk and veiled threats of her usual social circle any day.

Dani ignored her, fluffing Sasha's hair up before taking a step back for her final approval. 'Take a look. Tell me what you think.'

Sasha went to the seashell-framed mirror above the sink, wiping the steam from the glass—and froze. Dani had underplayed her talents massively. She'd chopped to shoulder length, yes, but she'd also included layers that framed Sasha's jaw and allowed for natural waves that were usually straightened or curled tight. She felt lighter, too, tempted to shake her head around to enjoy every moment of it.

It took her a second to realise what that opening in her chest was: *freedom*. She wouldn't be punished for cutting her hair this time. It was hers again, and it looked…*right*. She didn't look like a pop idol or action star Sara Chase. She was just a woman in a B & B room. She could have been *any* woman, features made softer and eyes brighter by the dark dye. There was so much possibility in that. So much space to reshape herself.

She smiled at Dani in the reflection. 'Can we go even shorter?'

'If it's what you want.'

Tears pricked Sasha's eyes. *What you want.* She'd almost forgotten what that really meant.

A gentle nudge roused Sasha from sleep, and she woke to find herself cold, neck aching from being propped against the car window. The gentle chirps of nearby crickets and the smell of pine car freshener reminded her where she was—*who* she was with—and she quickly clamped her gaping mouth shut, wiping the saliva from her chin. She opened her eyes into a blanket of darkness with Dani at its centre, a small smile on her face. She had most definitely seen Sasha drooling in her sleep.

'Rise and shine, sleeping beauty. Your palace awaits.'

Sasha stretched out the cracks in her joints, raking back her hair only to find it half the weight it used to be. And then she looked beyond the headlights to the villa ahead. It was beautiful, all white walls crawling with greenery and flowers, the fenced perimeter swathed by huge palm trees and shrubbery that offered an extra shield of privacy. The hills behind framed the scene perfectly, a deep arch of blue-grey against the starry night sky.

She waited to feel something. Relief, awe, excitement. She'd made it out, and nobody would find her here, and wasn't she lucky to be able to rent such a luxurious home?

Instead, she saw the darkness in the windows and the vastness of the rooms, and she wondered, again, how she would stomach the unending hours of nothing.

Tomorrow's problem, perhaps. Tonight, she'd just be glad for a comfortable bed.

'Sorry for falling asleep on you,' she said when she could finally gather her thoughts. From what she could recall, they'd been midway through a particularly riveting game of I spy before the sleepiness had hit.

'I didn't peg you as a snorer. *Or* a dribbler.' Dani flashed her teeth, then turned off the engine and unfastened her seat belt.

Sasha flushed with embarrassment, half tempted to retort that at least she didn't call random women's names in her sleep. She still couldn't figure out why she was unable to let that go, a million possibilities running through her mind about who Eve might be. An ex-girlfriend? A *current* girlfriend? A wish-she-was girlfriend?

Whoever she was, she was lucky to have captured Dani's attention. Sasha couldn't quite imagine what it must be like to be *wanted* by her. Being touched by her in a completely casual manner was heart-stopping enough.

Sasha got out of the car with more of that uncertainty. Dani grabbed their bags from the boot as Sasha climbed up the steps to the villa. Splotches of bright pink, purple and yellow flowers painted the front garden, the smell of fresh grass and honeysuckle greeting her. A light by the door illuminated the path, allowing her to find the security pad and input the code emailed to her by the host.

The interior was just as stunning, with vast windows offering a view of the pool out back and, beyond the rocky hills, the glittering moonlit sea. To her right, an arched doorway led to a living room with a massive flat screen mounted over a modern fireplace and two armchairs flanking a plush grey couch, and, to her left, a dining room that led to a patio of fairy lights and outdoor seating. A spread of delicious-smelling food had been left under glass cloches, from a platter of cheeses and grapes to fruit-laden cream cakes. Sasha plucked up the host's welcome note with a faint smile, reminding herself to thank them later.

She chewed on her nail, a habit that usually

had Gabriella slapping her wrist. By now, she was used to settling into new places, but this was different. She had no plans past this villa. No tour bus to whisk her away after a night or two of performing, no agent to keep her busy with work and social events.

She was on her own. Completely.

Except for Dani, who set the bags down by the entrance behind her. 'I'm going to make sure everything's secure outside first.'

'Okay.' Sasha bit her lip, watching Dani leave. In a form-fitting black T-shirt, the muscles in her shoulders and back were clearly visible until she disappeared around the corner. Every new part Sasha discovered of Dani was being stamped somewhere inside her. The ghost of her touch still lingered across Sasha's shoulders when she ran her fingers through her hair, and then there was the way her voice sometimes dropped—so gentle, so tender, that it stole the breath from Sasha's lungs. Upon first impression, she'd expected Dani to be all gruff stoicism, unreachable, but those moments proved there was a softness beyond the serrated edges.

Sasha shook her head and, after helping herself to a couple of grapes, grabbed her bag, marching up the spiral staircase. There were at least three more bedrooms than necessary, and she was too tired to scour them for a favourite, so she settled on the first one she reached. A fresh vase of lavender and carnations had been placed on the nightstand, rose petals on the bed. Sasha wished it were *that* sort of holiday. She disturbed the neat scatterings with her bag, then went over to the door leading to the balcony.

The warm breeze curled around her as she stepped out and propped her elbows on the railings. From up here, she could see the comforting lights of the village below. She wasn't all alone out here, even if she felt as if she were viewing the world behind a sheet of glass. Perhaps soon, when everybody forgot about her, she could be down there again. Find friends who didn't care if she was once a celebrity. Work a normal job that she could quit without having to upend her entire existence, and keep without having to morph into something else. Nobody would expect anything from her, and nobody would be able to tell her who she was supposed to be.

There, a semblance of peace finally found her, and she allowed herself a serene smile.

A rustle below distracted her from her thoughts. Dani, checking the fences surrounding the property. Once Sasha saw the flicker of red hair, darker than wine in the night, it was impossible to tear her gaze away, fixated on the way the shadows danced over her striking profile. Sasha sank further against the railings, a bout of hopelessness chasing away any calm. It was a silly problem to have, being attracted to her bodyguard—a cliché, even. But Dani was an ever-dangling reminder of all the things Sasha wanted, not just because she was beautiful and strong and able to leave Sasha tingling, but because she was *real*, from a place where people like Sasha were the minority. She moved as if the world would bend around her instead of the other way around.

She wasn't afraid.

Sasha was, especially when she felt the twinge of something she hadn't felt in a long time creep up on her. She couldn't let herself get attached to Dani, or anyone. She'd learned the hard way that she couldn't trust people to handle her with care, and her heart was too broken to let anybody near it again.

The door behind her creaked against the breeze, and Dani's attention flickered up to Sasha. Her features were sharp, serious, as though expecting a threat, but it all melted away upon seeing her.

'All good down here,' she acknowledged.

'Then will you come and enjoy the view with me?' That need to fill the gap of loneliness in her chest always seemed to win out, even after everything. Isolating to protect herself seemed just as painful as risking another heartbreak.

Dani tipped her head. 'I'll think about it. Let me check the house first.'

Sasha held her breath and only relaxed when, minutes later, Dani approached with heavy footsteps. Sasha tried not to look at her, afraid, if she did, she would keep wanting things she shouldn't. Still, Dani sidled beside her, tired eyes latching onto the rising moon. 'So, how does it feel?'

'What?'

'Freedom,' Dani said, as though it were simple.

Sasha gave a solemn smile, clasping her hands together. 'Terrifying. I don't know what comes next.'

'Whatever you'd like.' Dani's cheek creased with a lopsided smile. 'It's all in your own hands now.'

'What if I find I don't like it?' Or, worse, what if she found she didn't like *herself*? What if those problems she'd had before followed her, because misery was actually something that lived inside her, and she'd no longer have anyone to blame?

'What's not to like?' Dani sucked in a deep breath. 'Wind in your hair, stars over your head, horizon so close you feel like you might be at the edge of the world...'

Sasha mustered the courage to look at her, only because she was surprised by Dani's poetry. She was gazing up at the stars, absent. Always a bit absent, even if every atom of her body seemed to be on high alert at all times. Even when sleeping in that armchair, she'd been tense as a caged animal.

'Well, when you put it like that...'

'I wondered the same thing,' Dani admitted. 'After I quit the force. I didn't know who I was without it. Maybe I still don't. But it's not so bad, the not knowing, when you're somewhere like this, is it?'

'Yeah. Maybe you're right. It's a nice place to get lost in.' Only Sasha wasn't quite convinced. She'd spent a lot of time *somewhere like this*, and it had never been enough to save her before.

'I'm always right.' Dani dipped her head. 'You've been through a lot. It's bound to feel a bit weird. Just have to take it as it comes.'

'Thank you for getting me here,' Sasha whispered.

'It's my job.'

'It still means a lot. You still saved me from something.'

Dani crossed her arms, elbow accidentally nudging Sasha's. She didn't pull it away, instead rubbing her wrist as though trying to erase the harsh tattooed band around it. 'I don't deserve that credit. I think you saved yourself. Not everybody would be brave enough to leave.'

The words were uttered as gently as the rest, but they still gave Sasha pause. She felt ungrateful for being here. For running. For not enjoying what most people dreamt of having. And if not ungrateful, then at least weak for letting it get to this point. For marrying someone like Tom, for being so desperate to have friends that she'd looked straight past their indifference towards her, and for not leaving Gabriella sooner.

That Dani saw it as a sign of bravery was… well, incomprehensible, but also slightly empowering. Sasha's shoulders dropped a hair lower, as if she were shedding a weight.

Dani took a step back, as she always did. 'If that's all, March…'

'Yes. Of course.' Sasha nodded, jarred by the change in tone. Why did Dani keep pulling away? 'Feel free to help yourself to the food downstairs—and get some rest. You deserve a proper night's sleep.'

'Thank you. Goodnight, then.'

'Goodnight.'

Sasha's tongue scraped across her teeth in frustration as she watched her leave. Again. No matter how much she got of Dani, she was always left wishing for something else.

Something more.

CHAPTER TEN

SASHA DIDN'T RISE until eleven o'clock the next morning and, by then, Dani sat at the breakfast bar, head in her laptop and a half-eaten muffin on her plate. The maid had already been and gone, the counter filled with a buffet of breakfast food because Dani hadn't known what Sasha would want.

'Morning, sleeping beauty,' was her greeting as she shut the laptop. Only then did she actually look at the woman properly, pausing at the sight of her nightwear: a silken slip with a scooped low neckline, displaying a healthy amount of cleavage framed by lilac lace. The hem brushed achingly high on her thighs, barely enough to cover the generously full curve of her arse.

An unwelcome heat stirred in Dani, and she took a sip of water in a desperate attempt to douse the flames, legs crossing beneath the breakfast bar. With her new hair, Sasha was more beautiful than ever, the dark dye making her bright eyes a richer blue, lips a deeper pink. It was less the colour of coffee and more like the colour of melted chocolate, choppy brown curls sticking up at all ends. Somehow, the dishevelment only made her more endearing.

And more difficult to look away from, especially when her strap slipped off one shoulder as she scoured the buffet with a grumbled, 'Morning.'

'Oh, dear. Not a morning person, I take it.'

'Not an anything person today.' She spooned scrambled eggs and patatas bravas onto a plate with little enthusiasm. Dani supposed she was used to such first-class treatment—unlike her, who hadn't known what to do with herself as the maid had cleaned up after them. 'I was thinking I'd like to get some fresh air. Maybe visit the village.'

'You're not worried about being recognised?' Dani asked.

'Nope. I have new hair and my sunglasses to disguise me.' Sasha flicked the ends of her hair off her shoulders as she took the stool adjacent to Dani. She reached across the bar to snatch up a slice of watermelon, sucking the juice off her fingertips after the first bite. Dani hadn't been hungry before, but her mouth watered at the sight of Sasha. She chased the lemony crumbs of her muffin around her plate in a desperate attempt to stop noticing all the ways Sasha pulled unwelcome reactions from her body.

'And you don't think that the fact you're being

trailed by a bodyguard will give you away?' Even without her, Sasha's new appearance didn't feel like enough to disguise her. She might have looked less like a movie star, now, but there was still a magnetism to her that anybody could get lost in, proven by the way Dani's gaze followed her every move. If someone looked closely enough, they'd see she belonged under a spotlight, not blended into the background.

'Well…' Sasha's brows knitted together. 'You won't be trailing me. If anyone asks, we're friends.'

Dani tried to hide her snort behind a sip of water.

'What?' Sasha questioned.

'I just don't think we look like *friends*, love. I'm nearly fifteen years older than you and buy my clothes from Primark.'

Sasha crossed her arms over her stomach defensively, which only tugged her neckline further down, revealing the paler skin of her breasts. 'What's that got to do with anything? Are friends supposed to look like twins?'

'They're supposed to look like they come from the same walk of life, at least.' Dani got up to put her glass in the sink. 'Doesn't matter. I'll be there, not trailing you, if it's what you wish.'

'Well, then, what about if we say we're together? Like, a couple?'

'Even more unlikely,' Dani blurted, her heart

thrumming more rapidly. She turned on the tap to mask the uncomfortable silence that followed, then, when the washing-up bowl was full, craned her head over her shoulder to glance at Sasha. She was picking at her nails, avoiding Dani's gaze.

'Something wrong?' Dani questioned.

Sasha shook her head, stool leg scraping against the tiles as she stood. 'Nope. I'm going to go and get dressed.'

She left the kitchen, hips swaying with a little more ferocity than usual. Dani dried her hands on a tea towel, muttering, 'Damn celebrities,' under her breath. Had Sasha seriously taken offence? Dani had only been stating the obvious: they were polar opposites. If anything, she'd been complimenting Sasha's vibrant beauty.

Besides, why did Sasha give a toss? They weren't a couple, and they weren't friends. They were barely even acquaintances.

Even if it didn't feel that way most of the time.

In the end, they didn't have to worry about blending in. The packed markets teemed with life in every corner, making it easy to get lost in the crowd. Sasha's hand remained in Dani's as they ventured past jewellery stalls and fishmongers, snack bars and souvenir shops. Dani's other arm was weighed down by Sasha's shopping bags, all filled with clothes—apparently, she'd been travelling light and needed a new wardrobe, so they'd spent the afternoon traipsing between shops to collect every style and colour of sundress possible.

'You okay?' Dani asked. It was overwhelming even for her, and she wasn't the one afraid of being noticed.

Sasha nodded, her round eyes glittering as she soaked it all in. Her grip grew tighter, palms clammy, and Dani tried to ignore the way her touch seemed to radiate up her entire arm. How even her shoulder and spine, right down to her toes, were affected.

'We can go back, if you want.'

'I'm fine,' Sasha insisted, and dragged her towards a tourist-targeted market shop selling T-shirts and sunglasses beneath a stuffy striped gazebo. 'You, on the other hand, can barely open your eyes. Where are your sunglasses?'

With the afternoon sun beating down on them and Dani's sunglasses nowhere to be found, it was true that she was stuck in a permanent squint. 'Girona, probably. Think I left them at the B & B.'

Sasha gave her a dithering look and turned the rotating display around with an excruciating amount of consideration. She plucked a few different-shaped frames, holding them up to Dani's face.

Dani drew the line at the pair of pink heart

lenses, snatching them and putting them back on the rack. 'Is this necessary?'

'Very.' With a pout, Sasha finally settled on a pair of round shades. She slipped them on Dani's head before she had time to argue, pushing her hair off her face. 'These are the ones. It's giving Special Agent Gracie Hart.'

'I don't even know what that means.'

'*Miss Congeniality*!' Sasha's voice rose as though it were obvious. 'Haven't you watched it? Sandra Bullock in that movie was my bi awakening, especially pre-glow up.'

'I understood about thirty per cent of that sentence.' Still, Dani felt another unwelcome flutter. *Bi.* She hadn't been sure, before, if she'd been imagining those lingering gazes of attraction. Knowing Sasha might be interested in her didn't make it any easier to stop feeling that pull between them.

She tugged the glasses off and glimpsed the price tag with disgust. 'No, thanks. A bit above my price range.'

Sasha stopped her with a hand. 'My treat.'

'I'm not your Miss Congeniality or whatever—' Dani batted a hand '—and I'm not your charity, either.'

'Oh, come on. It's for my own benefit, so I don't have to see you go blind and wrinkled.'

'Yes, God forbid a woman of my age get wrinkles.'

Sasha ignored her, forcing money into the vendor's hand before Dani could protest, then stood on her tiptoes to slip the shades on properly. Her breath tickled Dani's chin, perfume permeating the space between them.

Too close. Again. With Sasha's glasses pushed atop her head, Dani saw the way her gaze dipped to her lips, even if it lasted only a moment.

'There.' Sasha's voice was breathy and smug. 'You and your retinas can thank me later.'

Dani tried to formulate a witty reply, refusing to admit that her eyes had stopped burning behind the shaded lenses—but any humour soon fell away when a tall man behind Sasha reached out a hand.

To grab her.

She dropped the shopping bags and sliced between them with more force than planned.

'Back up,' she growled. *'Now.'*

CHAPTER ELEVEN

SASHA'S FIRST INSTINCT was to cower, her heels smacking against a bucket of discounted beach towels as Dani shoved the stranger away. Surprise and more than a little indignation coloured his tanned features as he fell against the T-shirt racks, almost setting the entire gazebo toppling like dominoes. Her back had been turned, and she had no idea what Dani was defending her against. Did he recognise her?

The lens of a camera slung around his neck winked at her, and her stomach twisted. Paparazzi. They'd found her.

'Whoa!' he let out, holding his tattooed hands up in a show of surrender.

Dani's glare could have pierced metal. 'Back up!' she ordered again, though there was no 'back' left to go without knocking down the collapsing T-shirt rack completely.

Sasha shuffled closer to her, casting a wary glance at the shoppers who had stopped to take in the show. She flicked her sunglasses down, but how many would see right through them? Could she truly not even manage a day without being found out?

The man huffed out another breath, then pointed behind them both. At Sasha, or so she thought, until he said, *'Solo quería las gafas!'*

Sasha didn't speak Spanish, but she knew the word glasses. Mostly, because it was printed on the display of sunglasses behind them.

Not a pap. Just a shopper.

Dizzying relief seeped through Sasha. Still, Dani didn't ease from her firm stance. She whirled to grab the first pair of sunglasses she could reach—the heart-shaped ones Sasha had jokingly chosen earlier—and shoved them into the man's hands, then said something to him in Spanish. Even with ire radiating through her, that fluent, gravelly pronunciation melted like syrup on Dani's tongue, stunning Sasha. Now, she understood why they called it a Romance language.

The man stamped his sandalled foot, flashed Dani a vulgar gesture, and marched off with more sour mutterings under his breath. The vendor chased after him, reminding him to pay.

When Dani turned back, all her frostiness was gone, replaced by tender concern. She took Sasha's wrist gently. 'Are you okay?'

No was the answer, and it had as much to do with the heat in her gut as it did the panic she felt. The latter refused to fade, thumping like drumsticks through every fibre of her. 'What did you say to him?'

'I told him to stop infringing on people's personal space.' Dani threw a final glare over her shoulder, where the man was angrily ranting to a woman who was likely his partner. She was shushing him, her nod apologetic when she caught Sasha's eye. 'I thought he was making a grab for you. Turns out, he was just being a typical man, barging through because he couldn't wait for his sunglasses.'

When Sasha didn't reply, Dani's eyes darkened, and she tugged Sasha out of the gazebo towards the shade of a vibrant jacaranda tree nearby. 'Hey. You're okay. He didn't recognise you. It was a misunderstanding. I'm sorry. I didn't mean to scare you.'

'No, it's not your fault.' Sasha was glad the sunglasses hid her welling eyes. 'I just saw the camera…'

'I know. But I promise you, you're safe. Did you want to take a few seconds?'

Sasha did, feeling pathetic for her sniffles. Nothing had happened. Even if that man had been a photographer, Dani had handled it, hadn't let him anywhere near her. She'd known she was safe with her after last night, and this confirmed it.

But she felt heavy, thinking she might have to carry this paranoia around for the rest of her life. It had followed her all the way here.

Dani set the shopping bags at her feet, then stepped closer, cupping Sasha's cheek. Sasha's breath, heart, everything, stuttered, and she couldn't be sure how much of it was anxiety and how much of it was Dani—only that, when she concentrated on her, everything fell away, the world around them out of focus.

Her frown deepened. 'Deep breaths, love. Do you have panic attacks often?'

'I…' Sasha's brain worked too slowly for her to keep up. Was *that* what this was? A panic attack? She'd assumed it was a normal side effect of being scrutinised wherever she went, and she'd previously learned to mask it behind forced smiles and frequent bathroom breaks. But now, she saw her trembling hands, felt the sweat beading on her forehead and realised her body was barely keeping her upright. It wasn't *normal*; she couldn't *breathe*.

'Do you need me closer or further away?' Dani asked, voice barely above a whisper.

The memory of Tom's raucous laughter when she'd fallen over her own feet on a red carpet flashed suddenly. Gabriella uttering, 'Smile for the cameras, darling,' when paparazzi had invaded her own backyard to take photographs of her by the swimming pool. She thought of the cold coffee in her face, and how Gabriella had tutted at the stain on her clothes rather than the fact that Sasha had been humiliated to the point of hyperventilation.

They'd seen her the way Dani saw her now, fighting her own body. They could have helped her. Instead, they hadn't even stopped to ask how.

Not like Dani.

'Closer,' Sasha croaked, and then she was in Dani's arms, feeling small but protected—completely, inexplicably protected. Dani's breath fluttered in the shell of Sasha's ear. She wrapped her arms more tightly around Sasha's waist, rubbing soothing circles along her back, reminding her she was a tangible thing that wasn't about to collapse or float away.

'You're okay, Sasha. Take your time.'

Sasha squeezed her teary eyes closed, burrowing her head into Dani's neck. She smelled like lemon and spice, things that shouldn't have made sense together but somehow did when it came to Dani. Finally, Sasha's breathing steadied. She was reluctant to pull away, but now the wave had rolled over her head, she felt silly for almost drowning.

'Thank you,' she mumbled.

Dani brushed a strand of hair from the lens of Sasha's sunglasses, tucking it behind her ear. 'All good. Do you want to go back to the villa?'

Slowly, Sasha shook her head.

No, she didn't want to go. She wanted to stay here, where people took pictures of the sights rather than her. Where Dani's touch was a constant. Where she felt looked after for the first time in her life.

As they returned to the market, nerves still jangled through Sasha. The busy street had been an easy place to get lost in before, but now it was a sea of people whose current could carry her away at any moment. All it would take was one person to spot her, and all of this would be over.

She tried to distract herself with conversation, ignoring the way her limbs seemed to tingle with a threat that didn't exist. 'So, you're fluent in Spanish.'

'I used to be,' replied Dani. 'It doesn't come quite as easily any more.'

It had sounded plenty easy. *Devastatingly* easy. 'Is that expected of you as part of the job, or…?'

'Well, it helps, working for a European company, but no.' Dani chewed her lip as though she was deliberating whether to carry on. Sasha presumed that meant the end of the conversation, having learnt already that Dani didn't often volunteer any more than was necessary. But then she continued. 'Like I said, my aunt lives in Marbella. Her husband is Spanish, so he taught me. Thought I might as well study it at school to keep it up.'

'Marbella isn't so far from here. Do you visit very often?'

Behind her sunglasses, Dani was unreadable. 'No. Not nearly enough.'

'You could, while you're here,' Sasha offered. 'I'm sure I could keep myself busy for a day if you wanted to.'

'Honestly, I'm not sure I'd be welcome any more. I'm not very good at keeping up with them.'

Sasha didn't understand. If she had family who loved her, she'd make every effort to keep in contact. Maybe there was more to it, but still, she pushed: 'You won't know if you don't try.'

Dani only hummed, a non-answer. She was good at those.

Though Sasha didn't want to leave, she found herself too shaken to browse the packed stalls and gazebos now. She was about to admit defeat, tell Dani she was ready to go back to the villa, when a store with a red-striped awning caught her eye—or, rather, the musical instruments on display beneath.

She'd swerved before she even knew what she was doing, anxiety turning into anticipation. An acoustic guitar perched at the opening, propped up by the vendor's table atop a black case, its sides etched with a gorgeous swirling design.

'Hola,' the young, dark-haired man behind the table greeted with a white-toothed smile.

Dani answered for her with more of that honeyed Spanish, striking a conversation while Sasha traced the smooth wood. A longing awoke in her for her old guitar, the first one she'd ever bought—second-hand with the savings from her first summer job at an ice-cream parlour at the age of sixteen. At such a cheap price, it had needed more love and care than she'd been prepared for, but, God, she'd loved it. Wrote most of her first album with it, long before she'd known she'd ever end up in a recording studio.

'Give it a try, if you'd like,' he offered with a thick accent. 'She's dying to be played.'

Sasha smiled gratefully and strummed a few chords. He was right. The supple strings vibrated happily, producing a gorgeously smooth sound that left her yearning for more. She'd almost forgotten how good it felt, how magical, to make music with nothing but her fingers. 'Did you make this yourself?'

The man nodded and extended his arms at the instruments surrounding them, all of them etched with similar patterns. 'With my father's help. You play very well.'

'I'm a little rusty.' And a little bashful. She'd been surrounded by plenty of people who knew their way around a recording studio back in LA, but few who cared enough for the craft to put love and care into a business like this.

Dani nudged her. 'You should get it.'

Sasha hesitated. She felt, somehow, that she didn't deserve such a beautiful piece. Part of her was afraid that she wouldn't be able to produce anything good from it. Afraid she'd lost her skill, her soul, after focusing so long on things that didn't matter nearly as much.

'Listen to your girlfriend,' the vendor said, dimples sinking into his cheeks. 'She knows what she talks about.'

Girlfriend. It was almost funny, hearing that after Dani's adamance this morning. *Unlikely*, she'd scoffed, as though the idea of the two of them being mistaken for a couple was completely absurd. It had left Sasha feeling ridiculous for harbouring so much attraction, the blunt rejection a slap in her face, though rationally she knew she'd offered nothing for Dani *to* reject.

She waited for that same disbelief now; for Dani to explain with utter vehemence they weren't together. But Dani only smiled wryly, as if it were their little inside joke.

For the dimples alone, Sasha folded. 'All right. How much?'

The seller named a price far too low for the work he'd put in, so Sasha paid him double, chest warming when his soft brown eyes lit up. It had been a long time since she'd witnessed such innocent joy.

'Are you sure?' His face pinched with disbelief.

'Positive.' Sasha placed the guitar into its case, a thrill rushing through her. It wasn't her beloved old instrument, her first love, but perhaps it could represent new beginnings in the same way. Back then, she'd been learning guitar for the first time, lyrics pouring out of her in a steady stream of teenage angst. She'd never felt more connected to herself than, in her bedroom, scrawling chord progressions and half-formed ideas. Perhaps this was the first step towards getting herself back.

'Well, thank you very much.' He held out his hand, which Sasha shook. 'I'm Teo, by the way.'

'Sa—' Sasha stopped herself before her name spilled out. She might have looked different, but she didn't come across other Sashas very often. Better she disassociate with her old self completely, just in case. 'Samantha. And this is Danielle.'

Dani wrinkled her nose. 'No, it really isn't. It's Dani.' She shook Teo's hand, too, while Sasha suppressed a giggle over her bluntness.

'I hope to see you around, Samantha and Dani,' Teo said. 'Perhaps you might like to see my band play at the local bar on Saturday night?'

Sasha bounced on her toes. 'I'd love to!'

'Excellent!' Teo rubbed his hands together to display a collection of bracelets on one wrist. 'The bar is on the seafront around the corner. It's called Sirena. I think you'll love it!'

Dani's smile was forced, and Sasha already knew she was anti-bar. After bidding Teo goodbye, she led Sasha stiffly away. 'Is it a good idea, after what just happened?'

Sasha narrowed her eyes. 'I'm not fragile.'

‘I didn’t say you were, but maybe avoiding busy places wouldn’t be the worst thing in the world until everything settles.’

She considered it. Maybe Dani was right, but she wanted to go to that bar, hear Teo play. She wanted to be surrounded by people who sang and danced, not for fame, but just because they wanted to. Because it was in their blood.

She wanted to remember what music had sounded like before her voice had been muted.

Gripping her guitar case harder, Sasha made her decision. ‘You’d better learn how to have fun before Saturday night, Dani Sharpe, because we’re going.’ For good measure, she tapped Dani on the nose before strutting off.

CHAPTER TWELVE

FRAGRANT STEAM WARMED Dani's face as she stirred the wooden spoon through bursting cherry tomatoes and sautéed onions. It had been a while since she'd had the time, or energy, to cook anything more inspiring than microwave mac and cheese, so, with the maid taking Friday evenings off, she was making full use of the villa's sleek modern kitchen, the setting sun her backdrop.

It wasn't just the food that left her feeling different, *lighter*, tonight. Sasha sat out on the patio with her new guitar, strumming in random bursts. This villa had been an empty, lifeless thing when they'd arrived a few days ago, but the new energy gave Dani a sense of triumph.

Which was silly. Really, she had nothing to do with Sasha's joy, even if she had nudged her towards making the purchase. That she was here and not afraid, though, meant she'd done her job. For the first time since she'd quit the force, a kernel of fulfilment settled inside her.

The sweet sound of Sasha's hums reverberated across Dani's skin even with a wall between them. She stopped stirring over the stove, risking a glance through the window. Sasha was bathed in gold, white wisteria dripping down the trellis behind her, like something out of a painting. She had one leg crossed over the other, hunched over the guitar with a soft crease marring her forehead.

Beautiful. It wasn't the first time Dani had thought it, but it was the first time the acknowledgement punched through her with force. The first time that beauty had her wanting to run, because she shouldn't be noticing it. She shouldn't be *feeling* it like vines around her chest.

It hadn't been like this with Eve. She'd expected the attraction. They'd been similar in their laser-sharp focus and dry humour, quick to befriend each other as the only two queer women on the team. They had made *sense*. Dani had got her promotion only after they'd started dating, so she hadn't needed to question whether it was right or wrong.

What she had with Sasha was the opposite. It was dangerous. Dani never, ever wanted to give her heart away again. Never wanted to find something that she could lose, that held the power to destroy her. More than that, it felt like a betrayal to Eve's memory. Why should she get to develop feelings for someone else after allowing Eve to drown?

Sometimes, she thought maybe she deserved to be punished by something worse than grief.

She'd considered quitting her cushy new job, but the travelling allowed her time to forget, and she needed that just as much.

Just not like this.

The pan's oil spat at her, tearing her attention away. The onions had caramelised a tad too quickly, so she swore and lowered the heat. Not long after, the sound of bare feet padding into the kitchen had the hairs on the back of her neck prickling. She looked over her shoulder in question as Sasha hopped onto the counter opposite, a disheartened slouch to her posture. The yellow sundress she'd purchased from the market climbed up her thighs, high enough to make Dani's core tighten.

'Oh, dear. What's wrong?' She returned to the pan so that she wouldn't notice anything else that might provoke these pesky little reactions, like the thin material tightening over Sasha's hips and the way Dani's fingers flexed with the need to touch her.

'I'm just...blocked, I guess. It used to come so easy to me, but now I'm lucky if I can force out a few chords at a time.'

'Well, you've had a lot on your mind. Give it patience.'

Sasha hummed and hopped off the counter, hovering over Dani's shoulder, which did absolutely nothing to distract from her inappropriate thoughts. Especially not when Sasha gave a breathy moan, wafting the scent of fresh orange juice and floral perfume over her. 'Smells good. What is it?'

Dani clenched all over, half tempted to wriggle away to put distance between them again. Instead, her tension only drove her stiff back into Sasha's soft torso, warmth wrapping around her. She clumsily threw some bay leaves into the pan, feigning nonchalance without much skill. 'Paella. My aunt's recipe, although I'm probably doing a terrible job of remembering it.'

When Sasha didn't budge, Dani cast her a questioning glance. Cooking was calming because she did it alone. Sasha, with all her intent scrutiny and unwelcome effect on Dani, was ruining it.

She shooed Sasha off with the wooden spoon, because they were long past stiff small talk and forced niceties now. 'Go try again. You're breathing down my neck.'

Sasha's lips twitched with amusement, but she still looked at the pan with curiosity. 'Will you teach me?'

'What?'

'To cook. I'd like to be able to cook for myself.'

Dani held back the instinct to say, *no, go away before I forget how to breathe,* reminding herself that Sasha was a sheltered woman with a lot left to experience.

'Okay. You can pour in a splash of that wine.' She tipped her head to the bottle of Albariño, and

Sasha threw in something more akin to a tsunami than a splash. Flames ignited in the pan, and Dani yanked it off the heat quickly. 'What the hell, March!'

Sasha covered her mouth. 'Oops.'

Dani's poor onions were about to be charcoal. Supposing it would make for some interesting flavours, she threw in the saffron and rice once the flames had died down. 'I would ask you to chop some peppers instead, but I'm afraid what might happen when you're holding a sharp object.'

'It was an accident!' Sasha eyed the wine bottle. 'Can we drink the rest of this?' She was already retrieving glasses from the cupboard, so Dani didn't bother replying as she added a little water to tamp down the pan's remaining chaos.

'So far, you're not a very good student. Setting fires and getting drunk isn't really part of the culinary process.'

'Do you *ever* loosen up?' Sasha questioned as she poured each of them a glass.

Dani's jaw tightened. She might have been fun once, but that part of her might as well have died with Eve. She did things to get the job done, not to enjoy the process. Even the calming rhythm of cooking couldn't erase that need to create something perfect, and the fact that would not be happening tonight grated on her. Especially because she'd been hoping, secretly, to impress Sasha with something delicious.

She snatched her glass and gulped the wine, the tart notes of apricot sharpening her senses. 'Are you helping or not, March?'

'I'll take that as a no.' Sasha moved to the chopping board to begin slicing the red pepper, her uneven work creating far more waste than necessary—and far more noise as the steel blade hit wood.

'Come here. Let me show you a better way.' Dani turned the pepper on its side and peeled the knife from Sasha's fingers. She sliced down the flesh to avoid the seeds in quick, smooth movements.

Each one had her elbow brushing Sasha's soft stomach, making it impossible to ignore the way their bodies had unwittingly slotted together. Again. Sasha's eyes burned a hole into Dani's face, and Dani glowered at her knife, frustrated in more ways than one.

'You're not watching.'

'No, I'm not.' Sasha licked her lips and, finally, Dani gained the courage to meet her gaze. Their noses brushed, Sasha's wine-sweetened breath fanning over Dani's cheeks. When she leaned in, Dani stopped thinking, stopped breathing.

At least she could trust her body to do the work for her, hopping back on instinct before Sasha's lips met hers.

What the hell was going on here? What, exactly, did Sasha expect from her?

And why hadn't Dani pulled away long before they'd got so close?

Lonely. Sasha was lonely, probably not used to such a lack of attention and intimacy. She didn't want Dani; she just wanted to *be* wanted. A temporary fix to smooth out all the ways she was struggling.

Dani refused to let herself be dragged into it. If Sasha wanted someone, she had a whole village of strangers to go at down there.

She grabbed the chopped pepper in her shaking hands and returned to the pan, lips pursed as tension roiled though her.

'I…er…' Sasha stuttered slowly, as though only just realising what had almost happened. Her finger drifted to the place where their noses had met, as if Dani had left something behind on her skin.

Dani clenched her jaw. Jesus Christ, this was getting unbearable.

'Where do you want me?' Sasha asked finally, numbly.

As far away as possible, Dani wanted to bite out.

'We need the seafood,' she opted for instead, knowing the ingredients were on the other side of the kitchen, by the fridge.

Her heart slowed to its normal rhythm only when Sasha stepped away, and Dani wiped the sweat from her brow with the back of her hand.

She swigged the rest of her wine down in one gulp, tempted to pour herself another glass.

But that wouldn't be professional, and Dani was trying very, very hard to be professional. Even if Sasha threatened to unravel her completely.

They ate on the balcony overlooking the town, the sea a glimmering cobalt line in the distance. Dani was glad to have something other than Sasha to look at. They'd gone too far back in the kitchen. It couldn't—*wouldn't*—happen again.

Sasha let out a moan of delight at her first mouthful. 'This is actually really good. The burnt bits give it more flavour.'

Dani smirked and speared a shrimp. Sasha was right; despite the overcooked veg, it was delicious, the rice soft and fluffy, with the saffron lending the seafood an earthy undertone that balanced out the smokiness of the paprika perfectly. It had Dani thinking of Aunt Irene, the first person to introduce Spanish food to her. She might have been proud to know Dani was passing on the tradition…and awed to know it was a celebrity enjoying her food. Being this close to Marbella had her wondering, again, if she should find time to visit. She wasn't quite ready to confront all the apologies she owed for the years of radio silence.

Wasn't ready to confront the grief that waited in a place that held so many memories of her father.

They ate in content quietness, forks scraping and wine draining—Sasha's, at least. Dani had been cautious enough to switch to water. She lifted her eyes to find Sasha watching her curiously, as though she were a puzzle Sasha couldn't figure out.

Dani let her fork fall, setting down her bowl on the glass table. 'What now, March?'

Sasha only shrugged, kicking her legs out on the spare chair. 'Just thinking.'

'About?'

The column of her neck arched as she sipped the last dregs of her drink, and Dani wondered if it was on purpose. Did Sasha want Dani to keep losing herself in the way she moved?

Dani still felt Sasha's breath over her lips, her skin, the memory of their proximity refusing to leave her. How easy it would have been to yield, to kiss her. Taste her. Drag her hands up those bare thighs, slipping beneath her dress…

God, maybe all that wine in the paella had gone to her head. This wasn't her. She didn't *want*. *Especially* not since Eve. Complications like this led to reckless accidents, and she would never allow herself to be incompetent enough to risk someone's safety again.

Sasha placed down her glass on the table with a light clink. 'That this is the first good day I've had in a long time.'

Dani softened all at once, gut clenching at

the thought of all the times where Sasha hadn't been able to enjoy the world around her. All the days where those panic attacks kept going, because there was likely nobody there to sit with her through it. All the days where the person who frightened her wasn't just a man reaching for sunglasses, but a swarm of photographers or a mob of fans—or worse, Dani thought, that cruel agent and slimy ex-husband.

'When was the last time you weren't working?' she couldn't keep from asking.

Sasha swirled her fork around her rice absently. 'I don't think I've stopped since my first tour six years ago. There was always something. Even if I wasn't in the recording studio or on set, Gabriella would find something else. Photoshoots, premieres, parties. We have to assume we'll be forgotten if we let ourselves disappear for too long. I could work so hard, and it wouldn't matter if I fell off the radar for a few weeks, because by then, there'd be someone better. When you're starting out, all you want is to stay on the front page of every magazine, or the top of every chart. Suddenly, your entire worth is defined only by that, not talent or kindness or who you really are.'

The more Sasha spoke about fame, the more hellish it sounded. The rewards, no matter how flashy and grand they looked from the outside, weren't worth the hassle.

Dani leaned her head against her hand, elbow

propped on the back of her chair. 'It's a fickle industry. I suppose there's a reason people think you have to sell your soul to be part of it.'

'Except it doesn't feel like selling it. That makes it sound like you get a reward.' Sasha's eyes glazed over. 'You hand yourself over willingly because you think it'll be worth it. That you'll do something important. *Be* important. Instead, you lose yourself. And the worst part is, you don't even realise it's happening. You think you're doing great things, because when you're out there, you're treated like you're special. And then one day you're completely alone, and everything that people love about you is surface-level, and there's…nothing left.'

Dani ached to reach out, take her hand. Stuff professionalism. But moving even an inch would mean breaking this moment, and she wanted Sasha to carry on. Wanted her to feel as though she could voice all of the terrible things she'd experienced in a place that wasn't fragile.

And she did. 'I think it's why I can't make music any more. I don't think there's anything left for me to say. I'm empty.'

'You just said a lot. You could write about that,' Dani said softly.

Sasha blinked the tears from her eyes, looking down at her plate. 'Yeah, I suppose I could.'

'For what it's worth, I don't see emptiness when I look at you.'

'No? What do you see?'

Beauty, goodness, life, music. Sunlight. She rubbed her wrist, trying to think of something, anything, that wouldn't break this bubble between them or give away too much. 'Strength,' she decided on. 'Takes a lot to survive what you went through.'

Sasha offered a sombre smile. 'I don't feel very strong. But thank you, Dani.' She sniffed, then questioned, 'What about you? What do you do when you're not working?'

Dani scratched her chin. It occurred to her that, even for all Sasha's sadness, her life was far emptier, and nobody else had made it that way but her.

'Right.' Exasperation dripped from Sasha's huff at Dani's silence. 'Why do you do that?'

'What?'

'You stop talking whenever I ask about you. It isn't fair for you to know this much of me and then shut down when the conversation switches.'

'Maybe I just don't have anything worth talking about,' Dani bit back, defensive suddenly.

Sasha folded her arms, twisting away. 'Or maybe you think I wouldn't get it, because even though I've done everything to make you think otherwise, and even though you say all the right things, you still see me as some vapid celebrity who cares more about my fake tan.'

Dani chewed on the inside of her lip so roughly

that she tasted blood. Where the hell was this coming from? 'That's not the truth, Sasha.'

'Then why don't you have an actual conversation with me? A full one? Why won't you let me *know* you?'

'Why do you *want* to?' Her voice rose in frustration. She wasn't ready for anybody, let alone somebody like Sasha, to start tearing down walls she'd spent an age building. She'd never been one to volunteer her life story, but the last person she'd truly been able to open up to had been swept away from her.

'Because!' Sasha said, as if it were obvious.

'Because *what*? You need someone to fill your void? That's not what you pay me for.'

When Sasha jolted back as though Dani had dealt a physical blow, Dani instantly regretted her words. Wished she could stuff them back inside.

Sasha stood, lower lip tucked tightly between her teeth. 'I just thought we could be friends. I didn't realise I'd have to up your salary for that.'

'That's not what I meant.' There was no rule stating that they *couldn't* be friends. In fact, her colleagues got on swimmingly well with their clients. Marcus encouraged them to form a connection; that way, the client would feel safer.

It was Dani who was the problem. She'd lost too many people already, and she had no interest in reliving that grief.

Beyond that, she knew that opening up would

mean more than friendship, especially after that almost kiss. Their connection wasn't built on anything steady. It was more like exposed electricity cables. If they made contact, nothing would stop them from sparking.

'No,' Sasha finished, 'you just meant that I'm lonely and pathetic and that's not a good enough reason to like me.'

Dani rolled her eyes, and then hopped up when Sasha made to leave. She caught her wrist quickly, desperately. *'Sasha.'*

'What?' Sasha demanded, yanking herself away.

Dani gritted her teeth and repeated, 'That's *not* the truth. This is just who I am, all right?'

Sasha's steps were tentative, as though Dani were a frightened animal she was afraid to spook. She'd never felt so confronted by her own flaws before. Hadn't known that people expected more from her than what she already offered. It was easier to keep her cards close to her chest, where she wouldn't taint anyone with her darkness.

The way she'd tainted Eve.

'You don't have to be that way with me,' Sasha whispered. 'You can trust me. I want you to trust me.'

Dani nodded as, for the first time, she considered the idea.

'Will you sit back down?' she begged.

Sasha did, watching Dani carefully.

'I was on the force for a long time before this,' Dani admitted. 'I worked with the search and rescue team, and I found more people dead than alive. It wasn't pleasant. When we got off work, we didn't talk about it. We *never* talk about it. It's not normal for me to offer myself up—not to you, or to anyone. That's all.'

'Did something happen, when you were in the police?'

She shook her head, acid forming on her tongue. 'We don't talk about it,' she said again.

'Okay.' Sasha pulled a knee to her chest, skin tainted blue as the sun disappeared towards the sea. 'You know, I didn't talk about it for a long time, either. Mostly because there was nobody around who wanted to hear it. Eventually, it was so painful to bottle up that it all came pouring out of me anyway.'

There was nothing left for Dani to say. She wasn't Sasha, and she didn't have the luxury of *pouring*. She kept going, lid screwed tight, because there was no other option.

Warmth wrapped around Dani's hand, and she looked at her lap to see their fingers intertwined. Sasha squeezed, then went back to watching the sky.

A lump formed in Dani's throat. She gulped it down, sitting back in her chair. Though Sasha's touch provided comfort, she continued to stare at their hands for a different reason.

They were so different. Dani's were calloused, fringed with tattoos, whereas Sasha's were soft and manicured, if not chipped from nervous chewing. Together, they just didn't make sense.

Yet Dani's fingers curled tighter anyway, the embers in her gut smouldering to life: a complete act of betrayal against everything she knew was right.

Still, she couldn't pull away.

CHAPTER THIRTEEN

FROM THE OUTSIDE, Sirena was an unassuming haunt on the seafront, but when Sasha stepped in, she found it was anything but, with reflective iridescent walls casting everything in a blue-green glow. The bar was wreathed in coral and seashells, and illustrated mermaid tails decorated the menus. Sasha grinned, automatically looking behind her for Dani's reaction. As always, Dani was far more aloof, though her brow rose as though she might have been at least vaguely impressed. Her focus soon latched onto the surrounding patrons, poised to shield Sasha as she had at the market.

'You're off the clock,' Sasha shouted over the booming Spanish music. Even better: there'd be no risk of Sasha's songs playing tonight. 'As your client, I officially grant you the night off.'

Dani batted her hand. 'I don't think so, love.'

'Oh, c'mon. We're here to have fun.' Sasha tugged her towards the bar. Tonight, she had only one mission: to see Dani let her hair down. With the band setting up on the stage, nobody would be paying attention to Sasha, in her plain pastel playsuit, and even if she was worried, it wouldn't have mattered. They both had steam to blow off—and a lot of sangria to drink. She ordered an extra-large pitcher to prove it.

'Besides,' Sasha continued, fingertips dancing over Dani's wrist as she leaned in close, 'according to Teo, you're my girlfriend, remember? What would we tell him if he saw you guarding me like a soldier?'

'That I'm the jealous type?' Dani suggested, slipping onto the stool.

The sangria was placed in front of them, full of ice and fresh fruit. Sasha was quite enjoying her new, carefree diet. Gabriella would throw a tantrum if she knew that she'd eaten a cheeseburger for dinner today, not to mention the ice-cream sundae she'd devoured for dessert. She smiled just thinking about it. She'd forgotten that enjoying food didn't have to feel like a sin. With the lavish spreads prepared for them in the villa, Dani's delicious cooking and the nearby restaurants, it was easy to remember how much she used to love indulging in her comfort meals, even if it came with the occasional side of guilt, which she was making it her mission to unlearn.

She poured herself a glass, and then one for Dani with an insistent stare. 'I would rather you be the simpering type.' She batted her lashes to earn one of Dani's lopsided smirks. Sasha had found a weakness in her armour, one that she was getting brave enough to prod at now and again with teasing flirtations. After their almost kiss in the kitchen the other day, all Sasha wanted was to draw a reaction from her, to know if she'd wanted it as much.

'I'm sure you would.' Dani gestured towards the stage with a nod. 'Speak of the devil. Teo has spotted us.'

They waved at him, and he flashed them a beaming smile between tuning his guitar.

'Look at us, making friends with the locals. Maybe we should move here permanently, *babe*. I've heard there are good schools here, y'know, for our future children,' teased Sasha.

'Oh, God. Are we going to be doing this little act all night?'

'Yep,' Sasha replied, leaning against the bar. She loved it. All of it. It was too loud, with people knocking into her, even when she tucked herself closer to Dani's side...but nobody expected a thing from her. She had cut her make-up routine in half and let her hair dry naturally after showering. She could leave when she wanted.

She was enough, exactly as she was.

'Come on. Is it such a bad thing if people think we're dating?' she dared to question as Dani focused on a floating slice of lemon in her drink.

'I don't actually care what other people think.'

'Right. Because you're cool as a cucumber.'

Sasha sucked on her orange wedge, wondering what it must be like to be so blasé. Even before the fame, Sasha's emotions had always been teetering, imbalanced scales.

Dani was still examining the crowd, waiting for somebody to step too close. Maybe she wasn't blasé so much as hardened. Solid. Unwavering. Sasha couldn't imagine never talking about the things she'd struggled through, especially after a rough career like Dani's. Keeping it all inside that way couldn't be healthy.

The stereo music ebbed and a spotlight pooled over Teo and his friends. He introduced their band as Química on the microphone.

'What does it mean?' Sasha asked.

'Chemistry,' Dani supplied, the syrupy scent of sangria already lacing her breath.

How apt. The alcohol gave Sasha the confidence to sidle a little closer to Dani as the band began to play.

They were surprisingly excellent, an energetic fusion of British rock and Latin pop. Sasha was soon clapping along, cheering when Teo's solos came up, his voice as rich and throaty as it was when he talked. Some of the English lyrics were beautiful, too; far better than anything she'd ever been able to come up with, even in her prime. Soon, her heart was pulsing along to the bass line, and she was reminded of how it used to feel enjoying live music, before she'd needed VIP boxes or backstage passes. When the music had been enough.

She stole a glance at Dani every now and again, only to squirm in frustration. She was still scouring everybody *but* Sasha.

Sasha didn't want a bodyguard tonight. She wanted *her*, stripped back and in the moment, in the same way Sasha was trying to be. She told herself that perhaps if she was allowed it, if she could get this lust out of her system, they could finally be free of this stifling atmosphere between them. She allowed her bare leg to press against Dani's, waiting, but the only indication that Dani had felt it was the subtle feathering of a muscle in her jaw.

The sting of rejection taunted her, and she pulled away, eyes lowering to her drink. *She's not interested. Why would she be?*

Had she imagined the way Dani's eyes had dipped down to Sasha's lips in the kitchen? Or the way Dani's attention lingered on her body when she came downstairs in her nightgown?

Had she deluded herself into believing that there was something between them because, even now, she was afraid of being completely alone?

When the show ended, Teo approached with his guitar still wrapped around his body by a colourful strap. '*Hola, amigas!* Glad you made it!'

Sasha was pulled into a very tight, very sweaty bear hug, which might have been unpleasant had she not then witnessed Dani enduring the same fate with a wrinkled nose.

'You were wonderful up there, Teo! *Fantástico?*' she hazarded. If in doubt, adding a vowel to the end of an English word worked. Sometimes.

'Ah, *sí, gracias*. I'm glad you enjoyed! This is Raul. He writes many of our songs.' Teo dragged the shorter, bearded man who had sung most of the verses into the conversation, and Raul's eyes lit up upon being introduced.

'*Most* of the songs,' Raul corrected. Sasha didn't miss the way Teo's smile became forced. '*Hola, preciosas.* Teo did not tell me he has such a beautiful friend,' he said—to Sasha's boobs rather than her face.

Teo tutted, subtly nudging Raul back. 'Always the flirt, this one.'

It wasn't enough to keep Raul at bay, his hand finding Sasha's lower back. She stiffened, her skin crawling at his unwelcome touch.

Before she could so much as twist away, Dani lifted the wandering hand and positioned it back at Raul's side. 'Well, Teo's beautiful friend has a girlfriend. Tough luck, mate.'

'Oops.' Raul at least had the dignity to blush and back away a few steps, although that might have been down to Dani's cutting glower.

Jealous type, indeed. A thrill scuttled through Sasha. It had turned her off when Tom had behaved possessively, but this was different; it came from a desire to protect, not own. Dani knew Sasha's boundaries because she'd seen them broken not so long ago—but still, Sasha imagined it was for a different reason. Imagined Dani might not enjoy seeing other people touching Sasha because she wanted her for herself.

Teo shooed Raul away, watching him fall into a crowd of much keener women. 'Apologies. He's a bit of an…'

'Arsehole?' Dani completed. 'Sleaze? Predator?'

Teo winced. 'All of the above?'

'Lucky I have you to protect me, *babe*.' Sasha giggled, perching on Dani's lap, though her own stool was right there. Beneath her, Dani stiffened, then her hesitant hands slipped over Sasha's waist to keep her steady. Her hum sounded mangled, and Sasha worried she was too heavy—except, when she tried to pull away, certain she'd taken it too far, Dani tugged her back, breath jagged in Sasha's ear.

That familiar knot tightened in Sasha's core, the desire for friction burning through her. God, she couldn't remember the last time she'd been so desperate, so needy, over a bit of touch.

'How is your new guitar treating you?' Teo asked obliviously, scratching his mussed brown hair.

Now, it was Sasha's turn to grimace. 'Well, I

think I've lost my knack for it. Seeing you perform tonight reminded me of why I started, though, so I'll give it another go.'

'We play here every Saturday.' He leaned against the bar beside her, and she poured him a sangria, and then another for herself. 'Perhaps you should join us one week.'

'No,' Dani said immediately.

Teo's eyes widened. 'Don't worry, Danielle. I mean without Raul.'

But Sasha knew that wasn't why Dani was protesting. If she sang, she'd risk being recognised.

Still, she eyed the performance space. She missed leaving her heart on a small stage, not because she wanted to be seen, but because she wanted to play songs that made *others* feel seen. Because music was in her blood, and always would be, even if she was working hard to find it still, and one of the reasons she loved it so much was the connection it offered. A connection she'd been lacking for a long, long time. Would she ever get that part of herself back?

'It's okay.' Sasha patted Teo's shoulder. '*Danielle* knows I get awful stage fright.'

'Well, I would like to hear you play some time. Let me know if you change your mind,' Teo said, and then was called away by another one of his band members and a pair of gorgeous women twirling their hair in his direction.

Sasha smiled and turned to Dani. 'Thanks for covering for me.'

'Arsehole,' Dani growled, eyes still scraping over Raul from across the bar.

Sasha had already forgotten about him, and wondered what it said that being touched without consent was no longer a big deal. She remembered the first time she'd realised it was normal, when one of the producers at the label had squeezed her arse. The discomfort had stayed with her, but she'd learned to tamp it down. Speaking up only left her with fewer opportunities.

But she didn't want to think about that tonight. She just wanted to have fun, and a sleaze like Raul wouldn't stop her.

As an upbeat tune drove bodies to the dance floor, she took Dani's hand. 'Shut up and dance with me, *Danielle*.'

'Absolutely not. And stop calling me that.'

'Why does it bother you?' Sasha questioned. 'It's a nice name.'

'It's what my mother used to call me when I did something she didn't approve of,' Dani said stonily. 'Like get my dresses dirty on the football field, or kiss girls instead of boys.' She pointed at her hair. 'Or come home with a haircut like this.'

It was the most Dani had said about her family; enough to take Sasha by surprise. She'd been lucky that her bisexuality was one of the few things about her nobody had a problem with, but she knew that was partly down to the fact she'd been married to a man. People could pretend she wasn't queer as long as she fitted their idea of straight.

Another part of her that was free now she was here, with Dani. Maybe that was why she'd let her guard down so quickly with her.

'I'm sorry, Dani.' Sasha traced the tattoos on Dani's forearms, grateful she'd shared this, at least. 'Now I see why you don't get on.'

'Yeah, well, she got over the butch lesbian thing. Now it's my personality she isn't keen on.' Dani laughed. Sasha didn't. 'Look at that,' Dani muttered. 'I'm talking, like you wanted.'

'And the world didn't implode,' Sasha agreed gently. She wanted more. Wanted everything. Mostly, she wanted to kiss Dani until the rest was forgotten.

She was likely to get none of it, especially when Dani sat back to sip her drink.

'Dance with me,' Sasha begged again. 'Otherwise I'll have to do it alone, and you won't be able to protect me from all those sweaty bodies pressing against me...'

Dani's upper lip curled, and Sasha knew she'd made her point. Knew that she'd been right before: Dani *was* jealous.

She didn't need to be. She was the only person in the room Sasha cared about.

Sasha pulled her up from the stool, dragging

her over to the dance floor like a weightlifter towing a car, which drew a gruff laugh from Dani's throat.

And then she put Dani's hands on her hips, and Dani let her. She kept letting her.

CHAPTER FOURTEEN

DANI'S SELF-RESTRAINT DANGLED by a very frayed thread. She avoided eye contact with Sasha as they moved in time to the Latin pop music—or, rather, Sasha moved. Dani shifted from one foot to the other every now and again to match her rhythm. Her palms were placed on Sasha, all soft hips and silk fabric, her playsuit shorts nudging higher with each sway, and Dani wanted so badly to squeeze those gorgeous curves. To see Sasha's eyes widen as a result. To part her legs with a gentle nudge of her knee…

Just when she thought it couldn't get any worse, Sasha looped her arms around Dani, light fingers curling into the short hair at the nape of her neck.

'Oh, come on, Dani,' Sasha drawled with a lazy smile, drawing a figure eight around the top two vertebrae of Dani's spine. 'What are you so afraid of?'

It would have been infuriating if she weren't so intoxicating. Worse, because her eyes were glittering, cheeks flushed: happiness looked beautiful on her, and Dani wanted to make sure it stayed. It was her *job* to make it stay.

Just not like this.

Dani mustered a reply, shouting to be heard over the loud music. 'Other than the fact I don't dance?'

'You don't do a lot of things.' Sasha clucked her tongue and leaned closer, breath pooling in Dani's ear. 'I thought I was the one trapped, but you've built your own cage.'

Dani's grip grew tighter on Sasha's hips, and there, she got the response she'd wanted: a hitch of Sasha's breath, a parting of her lips. Only, Dani *didn't* want it any more, because it wasn't lust driving her now. It was frustration, the need to defend herself.

'You think you have me all figured out, March.'

'I'm getting there.' Sasha pulled away only for a moment, and then her knuckles travelled down Dani's ribcage in an agonisingly light brush. If Sasha weren't scrutinising her, Dani would have gasped, perhaps even moaned, for all the heat swirling in her gut.

But she wasn't playing these games. It was clear that Sasha was bored, and Dani was her only toy. She was testing their boundaries, trying to get a rise.

Dani leaned in close enough to make Sasha think she wanted to kiss her, nose grazing her cheek. Sasha's chest brushed hers, and Dani throbbed with a need that would never be fulfilled. Still, she considered it, for a second—what it would be like to lean in and let it happen.

And then she thought of Eve. The devastation of loving and losing someone. The way it had started a little like this: a temptation she shouldn't have, a break in her professional barriers, a thrill of the forbidden.

'No,' Dani whispered into Sasha's skin tersely. 'You're not.'

She prised Sasha's arms away with assertion, putting distance between them again.

'If you're looking for someone to toy with, you have plenty of people to choose from. Leave me out of it.'

Sasha's brow puckered with hurt, but Dani took three resolute strides back to the bar so that she could do her job—from a distance, where she belonged.

And if her hands shook as she pulled the glass of sangria to her lips, Sasha was too far away to notice.

Sasha spilled out of the bar an hour later, not before dancing with almost everybody inside, which Dani supposed had been an intentional way of making her jealous. It had worked, but it had also proven that Sasha was playing games, and Dani was better off observing from the sidelines.

Dani's fists balled into her trouser pockets as

she followed Sasha into the night, ire rippling through her, though she had no right to feel it.

'Is something the matter, Dani?' Sasha turned with a mischievous wiggle of her brows, flicking her head as though she'd forgotten those bouncy locks were gone. Was Dani getting a peek at who she'd been before, in Hollywood? Was this who she'd been for Tom?

Suddenly, her success made a lot more sense. That oozing confidence surely got her plenty of opportunities; Dani doubted even the most professional of directors were immune to that twinkle in her eye.

'How about you just focus on walking in a straight line?' Dani muttered when Sasha almost crashed into a lamp post. After finishing the sangria, they were both a little tipsy, though Dani had forced water into Sasha's hands before leaving.

Instead of turning at the corner to climb the hilly incline back to the villa, Sasha kicked off her heels and continued towards the seafront. *Not* the straight line Dani had meant.

'Where are you going?' she questioned impatiently.

'For a midnight swim!' Sasha set off into a sprint, the white sand clinging to her feet.

With a curse, Dani sped up to keep her in sight, Sasha's footprints leading the way. She shuddered to think of the sand she'd find in her clothes for days afterwards.

Sasha halted before the lapping waves, a striking silhouette against the moonlit sea. The sight was enough to quash any annoyance, any thought of the gritty texture in her boots at all. Dani wasn't sure how much longer she could keep pretending that she wasn't achingly attracted to her. Beyond reason, beyond every instinct in her body screaming that this wasn't right.

When Sasha peeled off her playsuit, strap by strap before letting the fabric pool at her ankles, Dani stopped thinking entirely. With Sasha's ample hourglass figure and effortless elegance, Dani couldn't look away. Wanted this current view painted and framed somewhere she could always go back to. Even then, it wouldn't be enough. There wasn't an artist in the world talented enough to capture the glint of moonlight on Sasha's shoulders, or the dimpled line above her knees, or the way laughter crashed out of her in tandem with the waves.

She turned around, revealing soft stomach and full breasts barely contained by her pink lace underwear. 'Will you join me?'

Dani pursed her lips and forced her gaze down. 'You know the answer to that.'

'Of course. You're more interested in your boots, I see. I didn't think you'd be so shy.'

'Give it a rest, Sasha.' It was more plea than snipe, pulse thudding in her ears.

'Why? You've already decided that I'm *toying* with you.' Sasha's thong dropped to the sand, and the desire to look at her again scorched Dani's every fibre. In fact, she wanted more than just to look. She wanted to take her here, now, without care for who might see. Without care for her *job.*

It was that that kept her steadfast, even as Sasha's bra joined the rest of her abandoned clothes. That, and the sound of the waves, which would always carry memories she'd rather forget.

'Won't you look at me, Dani?' Sasha whispered.

Dani's stomach twisted as she dragged her eyes straight up to Sasha's face, refusing to give her the satisfaction, the attention, she clearly hoped for.

'Is this why you hired me?' Dani demanded. 'Did you think you'd get under my skin?'

'That was just a happy accident, *love.*' Sasha dashed to the sea, squealing as the first waves slapped against her shins. Dani looked, then: at the way her curves bounced, at the indentations of her lower back, at the marks left behind by her bra. Her centre coiled tightly with desperate, nagging desire. Sasha was under more than just her skin. She was clinging to every inch of her like the sand between her toes.

'You can still change your mind!' Sasha called when she was waist-deep. 'It's a lovely night for it!'

Dani lowered to sit in the sand, clasping her arms tightly over her knees. The further away Sasha got, the more dread overshadowed all the other feelings. The loud waves had her squeezing her eyes closed, her recent dreams and the tragedy that had caused them racing through her mind. Eve would think her a fool if she could see her now, pining after an actress, a *client*. Then again, would Dani even be here if Eve hadn't drowned?

She couldn't let herself go down that path, peeling her lids open—only to find that Sasha was no longer visible.

Dani launched back to her feet, searching the shadows for some sign, but there was nothing but sea and velvety sky on all sides. Panic lurched through her, too familiar, too deadly, and it felt as if she were submerged in that icy cold river all over again, dreaming of a place where there was no escape from the water. It was everywhere, and Eve…

Sasha...

'Sasha?' she yelled, a ragged edge to her voice.

Nothing.

'Sasha!'

With an urgency that was second nature to her, Dani rolled into action, kicking her boots off and peeling out of her trousers before rushing into the sea. She barely felt the ice biting at her ankles, barely realised when rocks scraped the bare soles of her feet. Sasha's name was a heavy pulse in her ears, and nothing else mattered.

Except at the back of her mind: *Eve, Eve, Eve.*

'Sasha!' Dani's lungs constricted as she finally submerged herself, readying to dive. She had to find her. There was no other option. She wouldn't lose somebody else that she—

Laughter pealed behind her, and she whirled to find Sasha breaking through the surface, hair sticking to her cheeks and droplets dribbling down her face. 'I knew I'd get you in somehow.'

Dani's knees buckled, the current keeping her afloat because her bones no longer could. She'd thought Sasha was in trouble. *Drowning.*

She'd thought…

Sasha frowned, swimming closer. 'Dani?'

'Did you think that was funny?' Dani's voice was low, hoarse, from shouting. 'I thought you were *gone*.'

Sasha blinked the water from her eyes, close enough that Dani felt their knees brush. 'I was only messing around.'

Dani could barely suppress her snarl. She tried to walk away, back to shore, but Sasha grabbed her arm, fingers tight and cold as metal chains.

'Dani, I'm sorry—'

'What are you trying to do to me, Sasha?' The words erupted from Dani in a bellow. 'Am I a joke to you?'

'No, of course not.' Uncertainty quivered on

Sasha's bottom lip. 'I was just… I wanted to have fun. With you. I wanted… I wanted *you*.'

'I'm not here to help you pass your time.'

'God, you don't get it, do you?' Her face crumpled, and her palms moulded against Dani's clenched jaw, bodies pressed together by the relentless waves. Dani wanted to pull away, body still bristling, but that anger was brittle now. Easily breakable with the right amount of pressure. With the right amount of *her*.

She's safe, Dani told herself. *Sasha isn't Eve.*

But how easily she could have been. If Dani had learned anything since that day, it was that the water could be unforgiving. Eve had been the strongest swimmer Dani knew, stronger even than her, but it hadn't stopped her from being carried away.

It was *Sasha* who didn't get it.

'Dani, I *want* you,' Sasha repeated thickly, as though it meant something.

In Dani's mind, they were just words. There was no reason why Sasha could have felt the same as Dani. Even if it was true, she couldn't act on it. *They* couldn't.

'And I know,' Sasha continued, 'that you want me, too. I've seen it.'

'You have no idea what you're talking about,' Dani muttered. 'You've been through something, and you're not used to being alone, and you're trying to make this more than it is.'

Sasha pulled away. Dani thought that was it, that she'd finally accomplished what she'd needed to—

Until Sasha's lips were on hers.

This time, Dani wasn't strong enough to stop it.

CHAPTER FIFTEEN

SASHA DIDN'T KNOW how else to make Dani understand. She wasn't *toying*, and this wasn't a joke: these feelings were ravaging her every moment they spent together, whether Dani was by her side or a room away. In the villa, she lay awake at night imagining what would happen if she crept into Dani's bedroom, forever on the cusp of giving in.

So she did. She kissed her, Dani's damp hair curling around her fingers, in a frantic, final attempt to tell her the truth. And to force the truth out of Dani, too, because Sasha knew it was there, glowing under the surface. She'd felt Dani's eyes burning through her all night, and then again when Sasha had run into the water. She'd spent years around the wrong people, chasing the wrong things, while knowing deep down they weren't meant for her. *This* wasn't that. This was right, the world tilting into balance after years of sending Sasha stumbling.

Especially when Dani kissed back.

She was rough, unrelenting, gripping Sasha's

hips as though afraid she'd slip through her fingers otherwise. Sasha could taste the sea and the sangria on Dani's tongue, an embodiment of the exhilarating freedom she'd finally experienced tonight. Under the water, their bare legs twined together. When Dani's tongue parted her lips, Sasha moaned, palms exploring the flat planes of Dani's stomach. Even with the waves nudging them together, she couldn't get nearly close enough.

Dani pulled away all at once, breathless as awe and frustration warred on her features. 'What the hell are you doing?'

'Don't,' Sasha begged. 'If you didn't want me, you would have pulled away quicker. You wouldn't have kissed me back.'

'I could lose my job,' Dani whispered, and then groaned. 'God, Sasha. This isn't right.'

'It *feels* right, doesn't it?'

'No. No, it doesn't.' Dani turned her back to Sasha, rubbing a dripping hand over her face.

Sasha huffed. She'd worn her heart on her sleeve tonight, put herself out there expecting this rejection, but it didn't hurt any less. She would always put her trust in the wrong people.

'Fine. Then I give up.' She made to wade back, but paused when another bout of frustration hit her, treading back towards her. 'You know, I thought *I* was the coward, but at least I know what I want. At least I'm not afraid of letting people close to me, even if it means getting hurt. You're... You're made of stone. Or, at least, you want to be. You're not really fooling anyone.'

Dani turned and glared, water droplets following the hard lines of her stomach. Her vest top clung to her toned torso, bare biceps thick and tense, and Sasha was suddenly too aware of how naked she was. Maybe Dani was right. Maybe she'd been a fool, but it wasn't because she was looking for a distraction.

It was because this chemistry between them was more dangerous than anything she'd run from in Saint-Tropez. She'd seen glimpses of Dani behind those sturdy walls and knew, the same way she knew how to swim, or how to sing, or how to play the guitar, that there was something in her worth risking her dignity for.

All at once, that something appeared, Dani's eyes falling to Sasha's lips again. She slicked back her damp hair, tilting her head to the sky as though the stars might help her decide whatever it was she was struggling with. 'I can't do this,' she murmured.

Right when Sasha thought the decision had been made, Dani yanked her back and kissed her with an abandon that left Sasha panting. Dani kneaded Sasha's breasts, eliciting another thick moan as pleasure wracked through her. She rocked her hips, finding it difficult to remember the last time she'd felt so turned on, so infatuated. Perhaps never, because Dani touched her as if she were brand-new, mapping constellations across her skin as she inched, gradually, to the throb between Sasha's legs.

Sasha buried her head into Dani's neck, wishing the water weren't covering their writhing lower bodies so she could see every bit of their exploration. She slipped a hand beneath Dani's vest top, finding hot skin and, beyond her sports bra, pebbled nipples. Dani's mouth opened in a gasp that Sasha swallowed.

'Tell me the truth,' Sasha murmured. 'Tell me you want me, too.'

'I want you.' Dani proved it as she coaxed more pressure over Sasha's core in determined circles. 'How could I not want you? You're fierce as hell, and so mesmerisingly beautiful.'

Sasha arched her back as the pleasure in her centre drew tighter. Dani's mouth found her neck, licking up saltwater as if she wanted to sup, not only on Sasha, but on everything that touched her.

'You're going to ruin me,' Dani said. 'You realise that?'

'I won't,' Sasha promised. 'This is ours. Nobody else will know.' There was a thrill in the idea, one that had her clenching with the promise of climax.

'I don't just mean that.' And then Dani unravelled her, Sasha's toes curling into the sandy sea-bed as she grasped onto Dani, worried that she would fall completely otherwise.

The stars danced in her blurred vision, the world suddenly feeling much bigger than ever before—and yet smaller, safer, when she was in Dani's arms.

For Sasha, it wasn't ruin, not even close. It was repairing something that had been broken in her for too long to remember.

It was a revival.

Sasha woke with her arm draped across an empty space, though she hadn't fallen asleep that way. She and Dani had spent the night learning one another's bodies with quiet, gentle intensity, barely realising they'd made it back to the villa before they'd been undressing again.

Now, it was over. The morning sun crawled through the window, and Dani had already bolted. It would have been sad if it weren't so predictable. What had Sasha expected? Breakfast in bed? A shared shower? A handwritten love letter?

She'd be looking in the wrong place. She might have escaped Hollywood, but her nights still ended the same: with her lying alone, realising that she'd never quite be good enough for somebody to stay.

Still, she wished Dani would pull back those doors a hair further. Let Sasha slip inside, even if she was only allowed to linger on the welcome mat. There were too many rooms left to discover, and Sasha had a feeling that they were falling into disrepair. A little as she'd been before Dani.

Kicking the duvet off, Sasha threw on a dressing gown and made her way downstairs, finding Dani in her usual spot at the breakfast bar with her laptop open and focus narrowing her features. She didn't bother to look up at Sasha, which left a pang of hurt jolting through her. No 'Good morning, sleeping beauty' as usual, either.

'Morning,' Sasha said cautiously.

Dani mumbled something that could barely pass as a reply. Sasha poured herself a glass of orange juice from the prepared spread, though her stomach was in knots and she could barely take a sip. She sat on the stool opposite and waited for something, anything, but Dani remained silent.

'Are you really not going to talk to me?' Sasha asked.

Dani frowned. 'What's there to talk about?'

'I don't know, maybe the thing we spent *all* night doing?'

'Well, I think the good thing about that is it doesn't require much talking.'

'So, we're just going to act like nothing happened?'

Dani shrugged. *Shrugged.*

Ice began to pool in Sasha's gut. She'd made a mistake in letting Dani get so close. She'd thought her different, but now...

Did Dani intend to take from her like everyone else?

'What do you want from me, Sasha?'

'A bit of direct communication wouldn't go amiss.'

Dani swallowed thickly and slammed her laptop closed. 'Okay, then let me communicate this directly: it can't happen again.'

Tears pricked Sasha's eyes, and she prayed Dani wouldn't see them. 'Why? Because of your job?'

'Correct.'

'Is that the only reason?' Sasha tilted her head in challenge. 'Because there's nobody here to see us. Nobody has to know.'

'It's not worth the risk,' Dani said.

What Sasha heard was, *You're not worth the risk.*

'Right. Because it was nothing. You felt nothing, and it meant nothing.'

Puffing out a long breath, Dani massaged her temples. 'You don't get it. It doesn't matter what I *felt*. This isn't a holiday for me, Sasha. It's *work*. And you're making it harder.' Finally, she met her gaze, all steel that made Sasha want to run away again. Alone, this time. She'd been wrong before. Loneliness was better than this. *Anything* was better than this. 'I'm not trying to hurt you. I get it, okay? You're free for the first time in your adult life, and you deserve to enjoy that. It just can't be with me. Even without the risk of losing my job, I won't take advantage of you that way.'

'Take *advantage*?' Sasha repeated with a sneer. 'Am I so broken to you that you think I can't decide what I want?'

'I think you haven't had *time* to decide,' Dani ground out. 'Your head's probably still spinning from everything that happened.'

Sasha's scoff dripped with venom. 'Right, so I'm incapable of thinking clearly, too.'

'I'm doing you a favour, Sasha.'

'And I am *so* appreciative,' she snapped, jolting off the stool and throwing the orange juice in the sink. Some of it splashed onto her gown, leaving behind droplet stains. 'You're right. I'm better off without you tying me down. And I certainly wouldn't want to be an inconvenience for you and your work.'

'I tried to tell you,' Dani retorted quietly. 'I tried to walk away.'

Sasha slammed the glass down hard enough to make Dani wince. 'Yes, and then you had sex with me quite a few times, so forgive me if I feel like I've received mixed signals.'

'*You* initiated this. I tried to keep this professional.'

'So it was all in my head, then? You only slept with me to shut me up?'

Dani rasped out a mangled noise of frustration. 'No. That's not what I said.'

'You told me you wanted me!' Sasha exclaimed.

'I did!' Dani rose from her seat, fists planted on the table. 'But now it's over, okay? It has to be over.'

Sasha clamped down any retorts she had left, defeated. Maybe she had got it all wrong. Maybe Dani was just another person she couldn't trust.

'Fine,' she muttered. 'It's over.'

She stormed out, wishing she'd chosen someone else for this ridiculous job. Someone who she wouldn't have fallen hopelessly for.

Someone who wouldn't have let her.

CHAPTER SIXTEEN

DANI WASN'T SURE which she regretted more: her night with Sasha, or their argument the morning after. Her body still remembered how weightless it had felt in that sea, how she'd wanted nothing but to make Sasha feel good—and after, in the bedroom, how Sasha had returned the favour with a skilled tongue and intoxicating fingers. Dani hadn't expected her to take control that way, used to giving more than she took, but Sasha had been so desperate to touch her that she'd yielded.

Something Dani had only ever done with Eve.

Now, she missed the before, when they'd been able to laugh with each other. Even the easy silence while eating meals. Sasha barely looked at her at all the following week, though she played her guitar and sang. A lot. Usually in her bedroom with the door shut, an indication that Dani wasn't to enjoy it, though her syrupy voice echoed through the villa, bouncing off the tiles and carrying on the wind like chimes, all the same. She'd found updating Marcus over a Zoom call yesterday hell, certain that her Sasha-induced turmoil was written all over her face. But he'd been oblivious enough to hint that a promotion awaited her when she returned to the office: a supervisor position that should have sounded wonderful, but instead only brought dread, because it would mean staying in London more frequently. Not enough running.

She had considered coming clean to Marcus. At least then she'd be able to kiss Sasha freely. But then what? This job was all she had left, the only reason she'd still got out of bed in the morning after months of nothing but sleeping and drinking through her grief.

Self-loathing poisoned her thoughts as she dangled her feet into the pool with a sneer. She was a mess. At least after this, she'd never have to feel the pressing weight of being solely responsible for someone else's safety. Would never have to wonder if she was even capable of doing her job right. She was supposed to take care of Sasha, make her feel safe. Instead, she'd hurt her to the point where they couldn't even speak. The ripples of the water around her ankles drew her into a trance, one that felt like adequate punishment for her mistakes, because it came with its usual reminders of the day she'd rather forget. Eve would have told her to give her head a wobble if she could see her now, then given her a lecture that was more swearing than actual advice.

The sound of her name cut through that image,

leaving her cold. Lonely, somehow, because Eve wasn't here, and imagining otherwise was about the only time Dani felt like her old self.

'Hello,' Sasha called from the other side of the pool, voice frayed with an impatience that had become constant, on the off chance Sasha addressed her at all. 'Is anybody home?'

'Sorry. I was in my own world.' Dani blinked back into focus. 'What's up?'

'I said I'm going for a hike with Teo. He's on his way.'

'Right. I'll get changed.' Dani stood, drying off her feet with a beach towel.

'No need. Stay here.'

Head snapping up, Dani narrowed her eyes. 'I don't think so.'

'I don't need you today.' Sasha was all cool indifference. Was it a front, or had Dani truly driven her to the point of dislike?

Her fingernails dug tightly into her palms as she replied, 'I don't remember this being a part-time job.'

'He still thinks we're a couple, and I'm really not in the mood to play pretend.'

Right. Dani had forgotten about that small detail. She put her hands on her hips, deliberating. Leaving Sasha without protection wasn't an option. If she wanted to maintain her anonymity, neither was telling Teo the truth. 'You know I can't let you go alone.'

'I won't *be* alone. I'll be with Teo.'

'Who you've known for all of two weeks,' she couldn't help but bite out. Surely, Sasha knew better than to trust someone she'd just met, regardless of how kind he was. The fact his bandmate had tried to touch her without consent was the first red flag of what Dani was sure would be many.

'Which is, what, two days less than how long I've known you?' Sasha was quick to retaliate, arms crossing tightly.

It hurt more than it should have. What was Sasha implying? That they were strangers? That Dani could only be trusted as much as Teo could?

Had their argument erased everything that had come before?

She wouldn't let it show, schooling her features into tight determination. 'We're not arguing about this. I'm going.'

Sasha's glower was like an iron fist in Dani's chest. 'Fine. Whatever. I won't need you for much longer, anyway.'

'Sasha—'

She stormed away before Dani could choke out something, anything, that would keep her here for long enough to make this better. The thought of Sasha sending her away now left a chasm opening inside her, not only because it would leave her vulnerable, but also because Dani couldn't bear the thought of her facing her struggles alone.

And, not least, because she couldn't bear the idea that Sasha hated her so fiercely that she would sacrifice her own safety to get rid of her.

Dani kicked the legs of the nearest lounge chair, feeling for all the world as though she were finally falling apart. She should never have let it get this far.

She sure as hell should never have let herself fall for Sasha March.

'You two are very quiet today,' Teo pointed out, casting a sheepish glance between Sasha at his side, and Dani trailing behind. 'Are you fighting?'

'No.'

Dani replied at the same time Sasha said, 'Yes.'

Dani bit her tongue, glad when they came to a stop by a bench overlooking the village. The hiking trail was beautiful, or would have been if not for the impenetrable tension between her and Sasha. They were on a steady, craggy incline up the peak of the hill, sun beating down on them, leaving Dani's back wet with sweat. She took a long glug from her water bottle and offered it to Sasha, who hadn't brought one—or sensible hiking shoes. She wore her espadrilles, white linen shorts, and a cropped coral camisole, practically inviting heatstroke. Her shoulders were already turning a violent shade of pink, suggesting she was halfway there.

And she thought she could manage without

Dani? It would almost be laughable if not so ridiculous.

Sasha wasn't too proud as to turn her nose up at the bottle, though she refused to wear Dani's black cap when offered.

Teo uncomfortably scratched the stubble on his chin. 'Oh, dear. Trouble in paradise. This is why I do not date.'

'That's very smart of you,' Sasha replied, shoving the water bottle back into Dani's hands without so much as a glance.

'What happened? Perhaps I can help.' He balanced the sole of his running shoe on the bench overlooking town.

'Well, Danielle said that she wanted…churros for breakfast,' said Sasha pointedly. 'But when I got them for her the next day, she decided she didn't *like* churros any more.'

Teo appeared rightly puzzled. 'You are arguing because of food?'

Dani ran a tongue over her teeth bitterly. Was Sasha really doing this now? Couldn't she have lied, or at least made up a less ridiculous metaphor? 'Actually, I never said I didn't like churros. I said they aren't an *appropriate* breakfast food.'

'Oh, I see.' Sasha rounded on her, ponytail thwacking across Dani's face in the process. 'So when, exactly, *would* you like to eat churros, then?'

'I'm not sure there *is* a right time.'

'I am very confused,' Teo admitted. 'Churros are delicious at any time of the day.'

'I certainly think so,' said Sasha, brows rising into the tangle of choppy layers clinging to her forehead. 'Dani, however, is too set in her ways to try them.'

'Some things just aren't meant to be...eaten,' Dani forced out, and felt ridiculous for it. 'If *Samantha* was more mature, she would see that, really, I'm doing right by the churros for leaving them alone.'

'Oh, so now I'm immature, too.' Sasha let out a bitter laugh. 'Whatever. It's your loss. Churros don't need you, anyway.'

'This feels like a very fixable problem, *amigas*,' Teo interrupted. 'You could make Danielle cereal instead.'

'I agree,' Dani said, 'but Samantha is struggling to accept my choice.'

'Because you should have made that choice *before* I bought the churros.'

'Can we *not* do this now?'

Sasha's dismissive hand cut through the space between them. 'See? She's so stubborn. She doesn't *deserve* churros.'

Well, that was something they agreed on.

Teo dashed between them, grabbing each of their hands. The urge to pull away from his sweaty palms rushed through Dani, but she was trying to go along with Sasha and her little act.

Trying, unlike Sasha, to get through the day without any trouble.

'Guys, guys, guys,' Teo said despairingly. 'Don't do this. It is clear you two are crazy about each other. Is it worth throwing that away over *churros*?'

He linked Sasha's and Dani's hands with an accomplished smile. 'Please, don't fight. We can get through this together.'

Sasha's fingers wrapped loosely around Dani's to satisfy him, and Dani felt that sense of something awakening inside her again. A song that only played when Sasha was touching her.

'See? Love is stronger than breakfast food,' he said, draping his arms over both of their shoulders to pull them into a hug. Dani glowered at the horizon in the distance. Great. She was getting relationship advice from a twenty-three-year-old. 'Perhaps we can write a song about this bump in the road.'

'Perhaps,' Sasha muttered, then pulled away to swat a fly from her shoulder.

'Speaking of, have you been practising for tomorrow?'

'What's tomorrow?' asked Dani.

Teo clucked his tongue. 'Samantha didn't tell you? She's performing with us at Sirena!'

Dani reared back. 'No, she isn't.'

'Why not?' Sasha tipped her chin in defiance.

She really was going to ruin Dani. The answer

was obvious, but not one she could say in front of Teo, so she was stuck biting her tongue with barely contained irritation.

'It will be great,' chirped Teo excitedly. 'Samantha has already sent me a few recordings.' He leaned in close to Dani to feign a whisper. 'I think some of the lyrics may be about you. Very romantic.'

At least she'd been writing something. Dani knew how important it was to Sasha. Still, there was no way she could perform at Sirena or anywhere else. Dani had been checking the news daily, finding that a few celebrity news outlets had noticed Sasha's absence from social media and the Sara Chase film set. Clearly, Gabriella had been working on damage control, because no official stories had broken yet. Nobody was looking for her anywhere but the place she'd last been seen, and that could only be a good thing. Better if they kept it that way.

A challenge flared in Sasha's eyes as she lifted her shades; she wanted a reaction. Well, Dani wouldn't give her one.

'Is that so?' She shucked off her backpack to retrieve the suncream. 'Here. Before you turn into a lobster.'

Sasha snatched the bottle with little appreciation, squirting the cream onto both arms and rubbing it into her skin. A trail of goosebumps mesmerised Dani for a moment, the circling of

Sasha's fingers into soft skin leaving her mouth so dry she had to take another sip of water.

When Sasha reached her shoulders, she turned around, clawing in vain at her low neckline. 'I can't reach my back.'

Of course she couldn't. Dani took the lotion tersely, rubbing it into her hands to warm it before slathering it between Sasha's shoulder blades. She tried to work quickly, refusing to let her touch linger, but she still saw Sasha's muscles twitch as she moved up to the crook of her neck, covering the paler skin beneath her hair. Still imagined mapping every beautiful dip and valley beneath her camisole, dragging her thumb over the birthmark on the arch of her mid-spine. Kissing the dimples Dani knew she had over her perfectly plump, squeezable arse.

She pulled away at that thought, refusing to allow it any more space in her head. She'd made her choice. She would live with it.

No more 'churros'.

CHAPTER SEVENTEEN

DANI'S TOUCH LINGERED long after the lotion was massaged into Sasha's skin. Sasha tried to run from it, matching Teo's quick strides up the summit even as her calves ached and her breathing became laboured. All she'd wanted was some space between them so that she could stop harbouring such tangled, bitter feelings for Dani, but instead, they felt more tightly woven than ever.

'Watch your step,' Dani warned as the path grew steeper and rockier.

With Sasha's canvas flats nearly slipping off her feet, it wasn't easy, but she tried to focus on the good: the sun on her skin, the friendly company—Dani *not* included—and the gorgeous landscape surrounding them on all sides. Despite it all, Spain really was beginning to feel like home, or at least a place where she could finally be herself. With lyrics buzzing through her head at all hours and the guitar in her hand for most of the day, she was beginning to remember who that was. She supposed she owed Dani a thank you: the rejection had greatly inspired the beginnings of a few ballads.

'So,' asked Teo, breathless as he climbed a steeper stretch ahead. 'I don't think you told me: how did the two of you meet?'

Sasha regretted this silly act now more than ever. She was tired of having to talk about Dani as if the woman hadn't just scraped her raw.

She decided to opt for at least some of the truth, uttered with little enthusiasm. 'In Saint-Tropez. We were there for work.'

'Oh, very glamorous! What do you both do?'

'I, er…' Sasha stumbled over a loose rock, and Dani's hands were on her waist immediately, keeping her upright. Burning a hole through her clothes. With sweat dampening her hair and her muscles hugged tightly by athletic shorts and a sports bra, she'd never looked hotter. It wasn't fair.

That word rang in Sasha's ears again. *Immature.* As though Sasha were too young to want Dani. Their age gap barely registered in her mind, since most of her peers in LA had been at least ten years older than her. Immaturity was a privilege she'd had to abandon the second she'd made it big, too many responsibilities to shoulder.

'I'm a freelance writer,' lied Sasha finally. 'And Dani is in the police.'

'Oh.' Teo raised his brows. 'Wait, so you are British, but you work for the French police?'

Sasha scrambled for a better explanation, tugging at the information she'd pieced together herself. 'She was actually in Saint-Tropez for a fancy event to accept a police bravery award.'

Teo stopped to study them. 'Wow. What did you do to earn such a thing?'

'Nothing worth talking about,' Dani muttered, and pushed ahead with her eyes locked on the path.

Sasha gritted her teeth. Why did she do that? Push everyone away?

Well, she'd done her research. Since Dani didn't talk to her about anything, Sasha had searched the police federation database for last year's award winners. Dani had been there, under the West Yorkshire division. 'She risked her life to rescue a fellow officer and a missing child from a dangerous river current.'

Dani halted, her shoulders squaring. Anxiety fluttered in Sasha, one she tried to ignore. It wasn't as though it were some big secret. There had been a dozen articles about how Dani had courageously plunged into the Strid—apparently one of the most dangerous stretches of river in the country—during a heavy storm. She'd sustained injuries herself, but she'd spent over thirty minutes trying to revive the little girl they'd been searching for. She'd *saved* her. Thanks to her, the child was now in her first year of high school, her family grateful beyond words to see her thriving when she might have died otherwise.

'A hero!' Teo exclaimed. 'No wonder you are so enamoured, Samantha.'

Sasha was barely listening, her focus honed on Dani and her deadly stillness. She waited for some reaction, anything, but when Dani turned, it only left her cold. Dani's face was nothing but steel—and hurt.

'We're nearly at the top,' Dani said flatly, and then deepened her strides.

To get away from Sasha.

Sasha fiddled with the drawstring on her shorts, swallowing down the sudden nausea she felt. She rushed to keep up, to talk to her without Teo overhearing, but Dani kept getting further away, like a horizon line.

'Dani,' Sasha begged. It made no difference. *'Dani—'*

The slab of stone beneath her feet slipped without warning, missed because Sasha had been too focused on the woman in front of her. She yelped as she lost her balance, falling to her knees in a painful scrape of grit against skin. *'Crap!'*

'Careful, Samantha!' Teo said, rather pointlessly.

Dani whirled immediately, rushing to Sasha with concern crumpling her features. 'I told you to watch your step, March!'

'Yes, well, clearly, I'm incapable of keeping upright!' Sasha yelled back, and didn't know why. It just stung, and she was tired of only feeling wanted by Dani when she was weak, and the blood dribbling down her calf made her feel sick.

'Sit back,' Dani ordered, ripping the backpack off her shoulders and unzipping the main pocket.

'God, do you carry a first-aid kit with you, as well?' Sasha grumbled, mostly because she felt like a clumsy oaf. She hid her burning face behind her hands, then decided Teo's hovering wasn't helping, even if he was casting her in some much-needed shade. 'Teo, how about you go and set up the picnic at the top? We all need sustenance after this.'

'Are you sure?'

'Yes, I'm fine. It's just a graze.'

He seemed glad to be dismissed, scuttling away. Sasha dared look at Dani, who was sifting through her backpack as though she might find something other than water and suncream. Her lips were still pursed, a storm darkening her features.

'You're mad at me,' Sasha said. 'Madder than usual.'

'You looked for information I told you I didn't want to talk about. Yes, I'm mad.'

'But why? You did a wonderful thing!'

Dani poured water over the wound, washing away the stones, and Sasha winced. Still, the pain of her knee came second to the pain of Dani's silence. 'I don't get it. It's like you don't want me to see the good in you or something—'

'It's not about *you*,' Dani snapped. And then she untied the jacket from around her waist, clamping her teeth into the sleeve to rip it as if she were treating a bullet wound rather than a bit of a scuff.

Sasha put a calming hand over Dani's trembling one before she could tie the fabric around her leg. 'You don't need to do that. Please, stop. Talk to me a minute.'

'Talk about what? How *wonderful* it was?' Dani uttered. 'My…*colleague* died that day, and we almost lost the kid. Excuse me if I don't want to relive it.'

She tied the sleeve around Dani's knee—still gentle, even with all that severity. Because it was what she did: she took care of people. Why had she left the force? Why move her attention to people like Sasha, who had all the resources in the world, even if she'd needed her just as badly?

It didn't matter, Sasha realised. She'd overstepped. Again. And that night in the sea, when Sasha had plunged beneath the surface only to find upon emerging that Dani had been overwrought with panic… That was probably a terrible reminder of what she'd faced.

Maybe this rift between them was all Sasha's fault.

She reached out, tracing her knuckle over Dani's cheek. 'I'm sorry. I didn't mean to upset you.'

'Didn't you?' Dani snorted, but she didn't pull away.

'I don't want to keep fighting with you.' Sasha's throat tightened with the sincerity of her words. She was tired of this. Tired enough to give up the bitterness that came with Dani's rejection. 'Please…can we just go back to how it was?'

Dani's eyes fluttered shut, and Sasha saw it. Vulnerability, wanting, everything she'd been trying to shove down for the past two weeks. Everything Sasha felt, too. Dani's mouth tugged down at the corners, and Sasha regretted ever mentioning that award. Dredging up that pain…

'I'm so sorry, Dani,' she said again, voice wobbling. 'I didn't think.'

'I am, too. I've made a mess.'

'We both have.'

Dani looked at her for a final moment, then smoothed down the makeshift bandage with finality. 'How bad does it hurt?'

Terribly, Sasha wanted to say, but she wouldn't have meant the graze. 'It's fine. Really.'

'Okay.' Dani held out a hand to help Sasha up. It meant more than she could have known. 'Let's get back to Teo before he tries to give us more relationship counselling.'

Sasha chuckled and let Dani drag her up the very last few strides to the top of the trail. She could live with the rest of the pain if it meant they could at least talk again.

CHAPTER EIGHTEEN

DANI SAT AS close to the edge of the picnic blanket as possible, scowling at the shimmering sea in the distance. It was a beautiful view, but she barely saw it for the tempest inside her. She hadn't wanted Sasha to know about the incident. She'd been the first person in Dani's life who hadn't seen her as some heroic survivor, or the broken woman she'd become upon losing Eve. Now that illusion was shattered.

As Teo and Sasha chatted like old friends, Dani considered telling her the whole truth, not just the rose-tinted account documented in the articles and award reports. The thought twisted her stomach, made her mouth dry, and she knew she couldn't. She couldn't even imagine saying Eve's name. She never did any more, keeping it in a locked box, as though she might otherwise lose it, losc *her*.

'Do you not like sandwiches either?' Teo commented, nodding at the untouched lunch in Dani's hand.

'Must be the heat,' Dani said, then offered it to

Sasha, who had already devoured hers. Dani had quickly learned that she loved chorizo in everything. 'Here. You have it.'

Sasha shoved it away. 'You have to eat something.'

Dani rolled her eyes, took a pointed bite, and then dropped it in Sasha's lap. 'There.'

'This is what I have to put up with, Teo. So impossibly stubborn.' Still, Sasha ate it, teeth following the curve of Dani's bite. It shouldn't have felt intimate, but Dani's hands grew clammy at the sight. Would this be the closest they came to ever tasting one another again? Shared water bottles and sandwiches?

'The two of you must have a picture together,' Teo decided, pulling his phone from his pocket.

'Oh, no. We have lots already,' Dani said stiffly.

But Teo was insistent, fanning his hands in demand for them to cosy up. 'For my memories, too!'

Sasha smiled easily, resting her head on Dani's shoulder, and Dani forced her lips into a thin, upturned line—right as a breeze blew over them, disrupting the curls Sasha had just smoothed down so they fanned over Dani's face, bringing with them the smell of raspberry shampoo. It was instinct for Dani to reach out, tuck Sasha's hair behind her ear, forgetting Teo completely. Surprise shaped Sasha's lips into an O, the same irresistible expression she'd worn when Dani had touched her that night in the sea. Wonder and pleasure and that need to be closer, closer, closer.

Dani wondered when they'd stop feeling it. When the simplest of glances or touches wouldn't rewrite everything inside her. As she glimpsed a pink flush over Sasha's cheekbones, Dani feared the answer might be never.

'Perfect! So in love. Churros all but forgotten,' Teo exclaimed, reminding Dani that he was there, and so was his camera. He'd caught them getting lost in one another. Perfect evidence, should Marcus ever need it, to prove she'd fallen for her client.

And she *had* fallen. She'd tried not to, but it felt as inevitable as the tide beneath them.

'I shall send it to you,' he said to Sasha. 'Do you have your phone?'

'Send it to mine,' Dani said before Sasha was forced to give out her new number and turned on her AirDrop settings. When the picture came through, she paused. Teo had been right. The candid photographs showed no evidence of their arguments, only heat and care and adoration—not in Sasha's eyes. In Dani's. She barely recognised her own face, softened as it was.

Sasha leaned over her shoulder to take a look. 'Wow. You look like you might actually like me in this one.'

'Hm. Imagine that.' Dani was eager to put her phone away and drift back to the edge of the conversation as Teo returned to the topic of music. Specifically, how excited he was to perform with Sasha this weekend. Which wouldn't be happening.

As the sun dipped with the late afternoon, Teo's brows furrowed at his phone, a sound of disgust slipping from his lips.

'Everything okay?' Dani questioned.

'Raul causing trouble. He says he's quitting the band. Again.'

'Good riddance,' said Sasha, wrinkling her nose.

'I'd agree if he hadn't already left five times this year. It is never permanent, unfortunately.' He huffed and gathered his things. 'I'd better get back before he destroys Isa's drums, but feel free to stay.'

'Are you sure?'

'Of course. It will be nice and romantic.' He batted a hand, then bid them farewell and began the journey back down the hill.

With the new space on the blanket, Dani stretched out her legs, closing her eyes behind her sunglasses. It was exhausting, this thing between her and Sasha. Always trying to hide from her feelings, never being able to talk to her the way she wanted.

Sasha rolled onto her stomach with a content sigh, resting her chin on her folded arms. 'You know, I was so scared of this.'

'What, hiking?'

She snorted. 'Yes, but no. I mean the quiet. I didn't realise how loud everything was until it stopped.'

That, Dani understood. *All* she remembered after losing Eve was the quiet. People had seemed to whisper when they talked to her, as though afraid she might shatter otherwise. She would sit in her apartment for hours on end, her mind so noisy that she couldn't bear to switch on the television or listen to music. Trapped.

'And now?' Dani asked. 'Still scary?'

Sasha turned her head to look at Dani through golden-brown strands of hair. 'No. It's peaceful. I mean, sometimes I think…'

She trailed off, and there was another silence Dani didn't want.

'What?' she prodded gently.

'Sometimes I can think myself into a dark place. I wonder what sort of person I am, y'know? When people are throwing money and gifts and opportunities at you, you don't have the time to think about that. They make you feel like you're special. But now I wonder why I ever settled for Tom. I don't think I loved him, but I wanted him to love me. And I wonder why, for so long, I thought Gabriella was right to control me the way she did.' Sasha picked at the grass on the edge of the blanket. 'It feels like I was a different person, even if it was only a fortnight ago. And now I don't know who I'm becoming, but I know that

I'm not scared of the quiet any more, and that might mean something good.'

A strange amount of pride swelled in Dani's chest to think of how hard Sasha had worked to find a better life for herself. She deserved it, perhaps more than anyone Dani knew.

And Dani? Dani didn't deserve anything. She certainly didn't deserve Sasha.

With sudden resignation, she fell onto her back, looking up at the expanse of blue sky behind her shades. 'I think you're the sort of person who wanted what we all do: success, comfort, love. You were young, and they made you believe that those things come from all the wrong places. What matters is you realised it wasn't healthy and got out. *That's* who you are, Sasha. Someone who does scary things for the sake of a better life.'

Sasha rose to her elbows to really look at Dani, sunglasses pushed back on her head. Her eyes were glossy.

Dani gulped. Kept looking at the sky. If she did that, then she wouldn't have to acknowledge the way her entire body felt as though it were teetering on the edge of a cliff.

'I was in survival mode for a long time,' Sasha said. 'You pulled me out of that. No matter what's happened between us, I want you to know that.'

'I didn't pull you out of anything. You did it yourself.'

Tentative fingers sifted through Dani's hair, leaving her scalp tingling and body growing heavier. She couldn't remember the last time anybody had touched her so gently, and it meant she couldn't stop it, even if she knew she should. For Sasha, the rules would always be broken. Maybe Dani should accept it. Then she'd be able to kiss her again, at least.

Then she would lose everything.

'You can't play at Sirena,' she said, and knew she was risking pushing it all away. Maybe that was why she said it. A last-ditch effort to keep them apart.

But Sasha's touch barely wavered as she followed Dani's hairline down to her ear, tracing over her lobe before moving towards the hinge of her jaw. 'Nobody would recognise me.'

'They'd recognise your voice.'

'Then I'd just be a girl who sounds like someone who used to be famous.'

'Not "used to be",' Dani reminded her. 'I think it will take a bit longer for the world to forget Sasha March.'

'Why? Am I that memorable?'

She clucked her tongue. 'Now you're fishing.'

'Yep.' Sasha giggled, and the sound washed over Dani like sunlight. She wanted to hear it more, always.

She twisted onto her side with newfound bravery and barely resisted the urge to rest her hand on Sasha's stomach. 'I thought you'd never want to perform again, with everything you went through.'

Sasha shrugged. 'I thought so, too. And then I picked up that guitar and remembered why I loved it. I had to dull a lot of parts of me, but this…this is something I'll always love. Please, Dani. Can't we trust nothing bad will happen for one night? Nobody has noticed me yet. You even called me *March* earlier and Teo said nothing.'

'You hired me to protect you, and this is me protecting you.' She let her hands wander into Sasha's hair, to show her that she wasn't saying it to be cruel, but, rather, to keep her safe. 'Give it time. Please.'

'Okay. Only because you asked so nicely.'

They fell into peaceful quiet again, and Dani's restless limbs and loud thoughts dimmed enough for her to enjoy it.

'Dani?'

'Hm?'

'If you ever change your mind, I hope you know you can talk to me. Maybe we can't be… whatever we almost were, but I still want to know you. I still want you to trust me.'

'I do trust you.' It was herself Dani didn't trust. If she stopped, revealed herself, she was frightened of everything that might spill out.

Sasha sidled closer to nestle into Dani's chest, and there, with the way her heart thundered, she felt the risk of it more than ever. She was coming undone, thread by thread, and she didn't know how to stitch herself back up this time.

CHAPTER NINETEEN

SASHA BOUNCED HER knee up and down nervously as she eyed the stage, and then the entrance—looking for Dani. She felt guilty for sneaking out of the villa, but she'd done what Dani had asked and stayed home last night when she should have been performing. Imagining the exhilaration she could have felt had stifled her, left her feeling almost as trapped as she had in Saint-Tropez.

So Teo had invited her to a significantly quieter open mic night at a small bar named Santi's further down the seafront, and she hadn't been able to resist. Dani would probably forgive her. Maybe.

She didn't know if the anxiety was caused by her imminent performance or the fact she'd gone behind Dani's back, only that she wasn't sure she could sing with her throat this tight. Teo patted her knee, slipping two shots of tequila in front of her. 'For courage.'

She downed them both without giving them time to burn, then her gin and tonic for good measure. 'I think I've made a mistake. If Dani finds out I'm gone, she'll be worried.'

Teo frowned. 'I thought you said she was sick.'

'Right.' Sasha scrunched her face. She was struggling to keep up with all the lies tonight, another reason why her heart thundered to do something she wanted, needed. She considered telling Teo everything, but panic rose in her throat. She wasn't ready, even with it all weighing down on her.

So what was she doing here? What if someone *did* recognise her?

What if she had another panic attack, and this time, Dani wasn't here to keep her safe?

The dimly lit bar was much quieter than Sirena, but there were still at least two dozen people littering the tables. Even if she sang only the backing vocals with Teo as they'd agreed, how many might have already heard her voice on the radio?

'I can't do this.' She jolted up, disrupting the table of glasses with a clatter.

'What?' Teo's forehead wrinkled in bewilderment as he grabbed Sasha's hand. All she could think of was the yacht party, how there had always been somebody caging her in, tugging her back.

Until Teo saw her panic and pulled away. Not a cage. Not even close. 'Let's get some air, yes?'

His kind features smoothed the serrated edge of her anxiety. Those harsh memories weren't her life any more. She couldn't let fear and control hold her back any longer than they already had, not when so much joy and acceptance surrounded her now. If someone spotted her, she would deal with it.

She *could* deal with it.

'I'm okay,' Sasha said.

'Are you sure?'

She didn't have time to answer as a low voice filled the small space, fractured by the crackle of microphone feedback. 'And next up, we have Teo and Samantha!'

A few claps followed, though most people seemed to be here for the beer and conversation rather than the performances.

'What do you say?' Teo asked. 'Still up for it?'

Sasha took a deep, jagged breath and picked up her guitar. When she stepped under the hot spotlight on the small stage, the rest of the bar turned to darkness and she could pretend she was starting again. That this was the first time she'd ever been on a stage.

It was as though nothing had changed. She was just a girl who dreamed of making music, with nobody there to tell her how or when.

She was herself again. She was home.

Dread. That was all Dani felt when she finished cooking dinner, only to find that Sasha wasn't here to eat it. Her fingers curled tightly over the frame of Sasha's bedroom door, mind racing—

this time, not with possibilities, but with one single thought. *Gone.*

And then she saw the empty space where the guitar had been propped by the wardrobe, and that dread turned to fury. She'd gone off to play at Sirena. Careless. *Selfish.* Did she truly think she could sneak out and Dani wouldn't notice? If she'd wanted to go so badly, Dani had no power to stop her, but at least she'd be able to stand on the sidelines and keep her safe. It would only take one person to recognise her, and then…

As Dani dashed out of the villa, images of the sombre, desperate woman Sasha had been when they'd first met washed over her. Being dragged along by Gabriella and Tom, then sent stumbling off the yacht. Hounded by paparazzi who cared little about her boundaries. Coffee thrown in her face. Was all that really worth the risk?

Was lying to Dani?

She reached the seafront in minutes, the upbeat tunes blaring from Sirena growing closer, and she steeled herself—for what, she didn't know. She was too wrapped up in finding Sasha to think of what came after, professionalism left back at the villa. Now she was somewhere between the past and present, the feeling of control slipping through her fingers, the current tearing her before she could try to grasp the exposed roots of the riverbank again.

Don't go any further, Eve. It's not safe!

Dani weaved through the drinkers and dancers in the bar, ignoring mumbles of distaste as she elbowed her way towards the stage. She kept thinking she'd found her, only to discover it was someone else. A stranger. After struggling for what felt like hours, but was likely only minutes, she began to search for Teo instead.

It took her too long to realise that a band wasn't playing tonight, the stage completely empty.

She wasn't here.

So where the hell was she?

Dani could feel every new crack in her composure as she raced down the seafront, searching in every restaurant and store, even the beach. Nothing. With the feeling of hopelessness closing in on her, she could only yell out. She should have brought her phone. Hadn't even thought of it in her panic.

She hunched over the railings overlooking the beach, regarding the sea with something close to hatred. Somehow, it always came back to the water, even if not directly. Or maybe it was that she felt like the tide sometimes, unpredictable, quick to wash away anything good.

Though there were no tears, she pressed her palms into her eyes, fingernails digging into her forehead. She'd never thought she'd feel this scale of panic again, Eve the only true constant she'd ever had, even in grief—but here it was.

Here she was, falling apart, because Sasha was

probably out somewhere playing, living her life the way she deserved.

The strum of an acoustic guitar cut through Dani's turmoil suddenly, and she straightened to hear a mournful voice in the wind. After hearing it every day in the villa, she'd recognise it anywhere. A man's voice, *Teo's* voice, rasped over her. Dani followed the sound across the road to a row of storefronts and eateries. Only the corner was illuminated, a sign above the door revealing its name—Santi's.

Dani wrung her trembling hands, taking a second to compose herself before she stepped inside.

The atmosphere was much cosier than Sirena, less crowded as people hovered around tables and booths. Dani should have been relieved, but she wasn't much of anything. Dazed, perhaps, as she drank in the sight of Sasha under the spotlight, Teo at her side. The song was slow and romantic, Teo carrying most of the vocals as Sasha strummed. She smiled into her lap as she played, fingers working effortlessly over the strings, a gentle sway to her hips.

It was the most serene Dani had ever seen her, and she hadn't needed Dani to achieve it. The opposite.

Just another reason why they were so wrong for each other. She looked around to make sure nobody had recognised Sasha, but the audience was too lost in the music. Like a siren, Sasha had silenced the entire bar.

Dani was the first of many to be lured in.

She sat down on the closest chair, feeling raw. Cut open. She should have been happy to see Sasha in her element, finally unleashing her true talent on the world, but she could only feel the pit of fear that had opened when she'd found Sasha gone. How she always felt as if she were losing something. She'd tried so hard to run from her problems, but two weeks with Sasha had reminded her of all the reasons why letting someone in would destroy her in the end. At some point, Sasha wouldn't need her any more—if she even did now—and they would go their separate ways. What then? How prepared was she to let this go?

How prepared was she to hold on, when being with Sasha brought the same turmoil she'd spent almost a year trying to escape?

The song came to a crooning end, and a round of cheers echoed through the bar. Sasha's beam was radiant as she hugged Teo tightly.

Happier, freer, without Dani.

Dani left the bar, slumping against the wall outside. She didn't want to ruin this moment for Sasha with all her ridiculous fears and furies.

No. Sasha deserved better than that. Before, she'd needed Dani for a better life, but now?

Now, Dani was deadweight. Better off left at home. Just as she'd always known, deep down; she wasn't good enough, and she certainly wasn't meant to have a permanent place in Sasha's life.

CHAPTER TWENTY

SASHA CONSIDERED STAYING at Santi's, but she knew Dani would likely have noticed her absence at the villa by now and, besides, there was nobody she really wanted to share this joy with more than her. She left Teo inside after another crushing, triumphant hug and a few compliments from other patrons. He'd been blown away by their harmonies, joking, or perhaps not, that she should take Raul's place on lead vocals.

She couldn't pretend the offer wasn't tempting, but she wasn't ready to be tied to anybody else just yet. She needed her music to be hers again for a while first.

Outside, the cool breeze kissed her sweat-slick skin, and she sighed. The quiet, broken only by the gulls flapping above, was a reassuring reminder of all the ways she was finding peace.

It didn't last long. The sturdy silhouette hunched over the railings was instantly recognisable. Sasha had been found.

Her stomach dropped with guilt as she gingerly made her way over to Dani. When she reached her side, she received nothing: no greeting, no acknowledgement that Dani had even noticed her there. She supposed she deserved the silent treatment, but it still left her hollow.

'I didn't think you'd find me so soon,' she admitted quietly.

Dani's mirthless snicker cut straight through her. Okay, maybe she'd prefer the silent treatment now. 'Do you think I'm that terrible at my job?'

'We should have this conversation at home.'

Home. The word came naturally, even after years of Sasha not knowing what it meant. Was that what the villa was now?

Maybe. Maybe she wanted it to be.

Dani kicked off the railings and walked off without checking to see if Sasha was following behind.

Sasha gulped down the acid building in her throat, casting a final look at the bar where she had rediscovered herself, and then followed the woman who had made it all happen. The woman who'd given her more than she could ever know.

The woman Sasha loved, even if she wasn't ready to admit it.

Dani remained silent even after they'd returned to the villa, but Sasha could see the accusations brimming in the blaze of her eyes and the flare of her nostrils. For that reason, she didn't dare sit down, ready to defend herself if necessary. And she would, because even though she'd been unfair to sneak out, she'd do it again if it meant experiencing the exhilaration that came with performing for herself. She felt lost in every place she ventured except on stage. It was where she was meant to be, even if Dani didn't get it.

The bodyguard sat on the couch, fingers steepled and elbows burrowing into her thighs as she shot daggers at the bright abstract painting above the TV.

'Dani… Will you say something, please?' Sasha pleaded.

'Like what?'

'Whatever you want to say.' Would it always be like this, trying to coax something real out of Dani while she kept herself perfectly contained? It was like kicking a stone and expecting it to fight back. She just kept rolling further away.

'I don't know what that is.'

'Okay, then, I'll start.' Sasha rested her guitar against the armchair and perched on the edge. 'I'm sorry that I snuck away. I did what you asked and I didn't perform yesterday—'

Another vicious scoff fell from Dani. She moved to the window, turning her back to Sasha. 'Don't get pedantic about it, Sasha, and don't play games.'

'I'm not!' Huffing, she wiped her clammy palms on her daisy-patterned dress. 'I just… *needed* this.'

'You had this! In Saint-Tropez!' Dani's arms flailed in frustration. 'Why bother coming here to do the same thing you did there? Why hire me for this elaborate escape plan just to get up on stage the moment you find the anonymity and safety you hoped for? And why—' Dani twisted away from Sasha as though she couldn't bear to look at her '—ask me to protect you and then sneak out of the house like some rebel teenager?'

Tears built behind Sasha's eyes. She didn't know how to explain: that singing on a tiny stage with locals who didn't know her name was infinitely more freeing than the arenas and cameras she'd performed for before. That here, she got to wear the clothes she wanted and sing the songs she liked, and people clapped, then forgot, because she didn't owe them anything.

And that she'd wanted to do it without Dani trying to talk her out of it, because hiding away wasn't the life she'd sacrificed everything for.

'I want my life to be mine again!' she shouted instead, and knew it wasn't nearly the explanation Dani deserved.

'Then what am I doing here?' Dani asked. 'Why am I still trailing you like your loyal guard dog if you don't want me here?'

'I... I *do* want you here,' Sasha whispered. 'Of course I do.'

'For what? Because at the moment, it feels like you just don't want to be alone, and I'm sick of being a toy you pick up and throw away whenever you please!'

Sasha's nails sank deeper into the suede upholstery. 'Why do you always make out like I'm playing games with you? Do you really think that's what this is? If anything, *you're* the one throwing me away!'

A muscle in Dani's jaw ticced, a weak link in her steel. Sasha knew she had to keep chipping before she lost her completely. Not for her protection, or because she didn't want to be alone, but because she needed Dani in the same way an instrument needed tuning. Without her, she wouldn't be right.

Without her, Sasha's heart would be infinitely more broken than when they'd met.

She went to her by the window, forcing Dani's solid body to turn around so she could cup her cheek. Sasha was surprised to find more cracks: glassy eyes, a quiver to her mouth. It was the most emotion Sasha had ever seen from Dani, and it hurt to think she'd put it there.

'You know how I feel about you. You have to.' She gulped. 'I wish you'd heard me play tonight. Then you'd know.'

'I did hear you. And I saw you. How happy you were.'

'Because of you. Because you brought me here and helped me see I don't need money or fame to feel important. It's enough to play to a room full of people and then come home to you.'

Dani tried to pry herself away, but Sasha wouldn't let her. Not this time. They couldn't keep running from this. Sasha couldn't keep trying to guess what Dani was really thinking, not when she looked this crestfallen.

'Please, Dani. I needed this for me, but now… Now I need *you*.'

'And what about what I need?' Dani's voice cracked. 'Did you stop to think how terrified I'd be to find you gone, and not in Sirena? I didn't know where you *were*, Sasha.'

Oh.

No, she hadn't stopped to think, mostly because Dani had made it clear that there was nothing to think about. Even if her actions had spoken louder, there was still that rejection hanging around Sasha's shoulders.

She still wasn't sure that she deserved to be more than just Dani's client.

Dani forced Sasha's hands back to her sides, a new flame flickering on her features. 'If something had happened, I wouldn't know. I wouldn't be able to help you. You're the one who told me, who showed me, that you aren't safe in this world, but I can't protect you if I don't know where you are.'

'I didn't… I didn't think…'

'No, you didn't think. You never think. You

have no idea—' Dani stopped herself, rolling her shoulders as though she was battling against something. Words fighting to come out.

For once, Sasha wished she'd let them. 'What? Talk to me. *Tell* me.'

Dani didn't.

Sasha's vision dotted with frustration. 'I can't keep doing this. I can't keep having half of a conversation with you.'

'Then don't. Send me away. Tell Marcus you don't need me any more.'

Sasha's heart wrenched, but she couldn't keep doing this. It was exhausting to be the only one who said what she really felt. She'd done it before with Tom, only to get brushed off with crude jokes or demeaning laughter. She'd had to beg for his love and, in the end, it hadn't been worth it. Dani wasn't cruel, but a wall was still a wall, regardless of its materials.

'Is that what you want?' Sasha questioned.

Nothing.

'Answer me, Dani, or I swear, I'm done. Do you want this to be over? Do you want to leave me?'

'Of course not,' she snapped.

'Then tell me something *real*. Tell me why you're so upset so that I know, so that I can help!'

'I was so worried that I couldn't breathe!'

It tumbled out of Dani all at once, leaving Sasha in stunned silence. A croak of something like pain left Dani, likely a curse, but it was too mangled for Sasha to decipher it.

'And that?' Dani continued. 'That's not my job. I'm supposed to be calm, rational, so that I can take care of you properly. When I *care* this much, I can't keep you safe. I can't do my job, because if something happened to you…' Dani's face tugged with resignation as, finally, she met Sasha's eye. 'If something happened to you, it would wreck me. And it wouldn't be the first time that feeling would cost me everything.'

An ache lanced through Sasha as what she'd wondered, feared, was confirmed. Dani had lost somebody. It wasn't just about the little girl she'd saved, or the colleague she hadn't. Or maybe it was. Maybe the Eve she called to in her dreams was also the police officer who had died in the Strid.

Somehow, Sasha was the one crying even as Dani's shoulders trembled with the weight of whatever she'd been carrying. God, what had she been carrying? Why hadn't Sasha seen it?

'Dani…' Sasha began softly—but whatever she was about to say was swallowed by Dani's kiss, spine crashing against the wall as, finally, Dani stopped fighting enough for both of them.

CHAPTER TWENTY-ONE

DANI KNEW THERE would be no coming back from this. Not this time. There would be no morning after, spent trying to wipe away these feelings for one another. Sasha had all of her, and it had been that way from the day they'd met. There was nothing that could stop Dani from wanting, *needing*, so she didn't try to hold back this time, kissing her as though she really was hers.

Like in the sea, their mouths moved hungrily, and Dani's core was already tightening with a white-hot need that went beyond anything describable. When Sasha fisted Dani's hair with new determination, Dani moaned into her mouth. She tasted tears and wasn't sure which of them they belonged to, only that if she kept Sasha this close, she'd never lose her, and that had to be worth whatever else came from this. Had to be worth risking her job, risking everything.

She dragged her hands up Sasha's thighs, revelling in the way Sasha arched in response.

'These sundresses…do you have any idea what

they do to me?' Dani whispered. 'Knowing if I just reached underneath…'

Another gasp as she found Sasha's underwear, Dani's finger teasing the lace edge before crawling up to the jut of her stomach. She was warm and soft, everything Dani wasn't—but she wanted to be. For her.

But then Sasha was pushing her away, a new wrinkle between her brows. Her lips were already swollen. 'Promise me you won't shut down on me again. I can't take it, Dani. I can't keep wondering how you feel about me.'

Dani traced the delicate heart shape of her pout. 'What do you need from me, love?' She nuzzled her nose against Sasha's neck, smelling sweat and salt and suncream: summer incarnate. 'Do you need me to tell you that you're all I think about? That you're so beautiful I can't think straight? That all I want is to make you happy and keep you safe?'

'Only if it's true,' Sasha replied with a wispy stammer.

'Of course it's true. Do you think I'd be doing this if it wasn't?' She grazed Sasha's damp cheek, desperate to show how sincere she was. 'Do you think I'd be this much of a mess for anyone else?'

To prove it, she lowered to her knees: at her mercy. She had finally, completely given in. Sasha could have whatever parts of Dani she wanted, and Dani would gladly give them up.

'This isn't a game to me,' Sasha said. 'I'm falling in love with you, Dani.'

Emotion, astonishment, fear, all clogged in Dani's throat. She pressed a kiss above Sasha's knee, earning a twitch of anticipation. She couldn't say it back, but she felt it all the same. And when she looked up at Sasha with more of that wild adoration in her eyes, she thought maybe Sasha saw it. So, she tugged down her underwear and threw it behind her, tilting her head in asking. Sasha draped a leg over Dani's shoulder, and Dani's core began to throb in time to her racing heart. She kissed a wobbly line up Sasha's inner thigh, earning noises of pleasure she hadn't been lucky enough, slow enough, to hear the first time. Sasha bunched her skirt in her hands to watch Dani ravish her through hooded eyes, perhaps the most beautiful sight Dani had ever seen. With her this close, that fear that plagued Dani day in, day out, couldn't touch her. As long as Sasha was here, Dani could breathe again.

The world fell away when she dipped between Sasha's legs and tried to show her the things she couldn't yet say, holding her hips steady as Sasha came undone against her tongue.

As they both came undone.

Later, they lay on the rug in front of the unlit fireplace, covered in blankets and sweat and each other. Dani sifted a hand through Sasha's hair and tried not to think about tomorrow. She would have to tell Marcus the truth. She couldn't go on pretending. But that also meant she would have to stop holding back with Sasha. She owed her the same vulnerability that Sasha had given her from the very start, even if it was difficult to face. So difficult that she could already feel the last of her resolve crumbling.

She supposed it was time to answer Sasha's questions, and there was only one place she could think of to start.

'You asked me who Eve was,' she said.

Sasha hummed against her chest, shifting to get a better view of Dani. Her eyes were hazy, and Dani considered putting it off to keep this moment untainted—but she wasn't sure she'd be able to get a second chance at this. She knew how easily she might retreat if she thought about it for too long.

She needed to *stop* thinking about it.

'She was the colleague who drowned. We were together. Secretly. It wasn't exactly a good idea to date in the workplace and, I swear, I'm not trying to make it a habit…'

Sasha huffed out a soft laugh, resting her chin in the valley of Dani's sternum. 'I'll take your word for it.'

A smile ghosted across Dani's face. 'I'd had feelings for her for years, but we were still quite new. So new, I hadn't considered I might lose her.' A tear trickled down the crook of Dani's nose, and Sasha brushed it away gently, listening with a patient intensity that made Dani want to shy away. Funny how everyone thought her so strong, when she was anything but.

'It wasn't safe to go into the water in a storm, but the little girl had only just fallen in, so it was either taking a risk to get her out alive or waiting and losing her. Both Eve and I couldn't bear the second option, but I was in charge. I wasn't only responsible for the civilian, but my team, too. And I failed her.'

Everything in her recoiled against the memories. She was surprised to find she could utter the words after letting the thoughts torment her for so long, never spoken aloud.

'Dan,' Sasha whispered, all sympathy and understanding. 'You were put in an impossible situation. It wasn't your fault.'

But in Dani's mind, it was. 'When we got to the worst part, I told Eve to get out of the water. I told her I'd do it alone. It wasn't worth risking both of us. But Eve was so stubborn, a bit like you, and she carried on anyway, even when I begged her. She found the girl, but they were both going under quickly. I had to choose. By the time I got the kid out onto the embankment, Eve was gone. Got back in the water, thinking I could find her. I could save them both. But then another colleague pulled me out, said she'd already been pulled away by the current. It was too late.'

'And after all that, you were still giving CPR for over half an hour?' Sasha marvelled.

'They kept telling me to stop, the kid was gone, but I couldn't. It couldn't all be for nothing. I broke her rib. I wasn't even thinking about her. I was in autopilot. What does that say about me?'

'That you lost someone you loved and didn't have time to process it,' Sasha answered without missing a beat. 'That you saved a little girl, gave her a future. You deserved that award.'

Dani turned her head away at that, mouth curling bitterly. 'Don't say that.'

'Dani—'

'It should have been me. If anyone had to die on the job, it should have been the officer in charge. Eve had so much more to live for.'

Sasha narrowed her eyes—not with judgement, only the desperate need to understand. 'And you didn't?'

'I was already...' Dani swallowed thickly, throat like sandpaper. 'I was already a hopeless case before her. I was grieving my dad. He was why I joined the force, and maybe I got a bit more reckless after he passed. Maybe I forgot that my team depended on me. I wasn't brave, Sasha. I wasn't a hero. I was just lucky. Eve wasn't. *She* was the brave one, for carrying on even when I told her not to. It got her killed. And I keep thinking that if I was just her boss, if we hadn't been dating, she might have taken my orders seriously and got out in time.'

'You can't think like that,' Sasha said. 'You'll drive yourself mad, go round in circles. If Eve had got out, the girl wouldn't have survived, and I know you'd carry that with you, too.'

'I carry around everything I've lost,' Dani admitted. 'That's why I can't lose you.'

'You won't lose me. You're stuck with me now.'

Sasha began drawing soothing circles against Dani's ribs. She'd never felt so seen before. Never bared her soul like this. Their legs tangled closer beneath the blanket, Dani drawing Sasha tighter, as though it might keep her here.

'Dani,' Sasha said again.

Dani hummed, tired and devastated and wondering why Sasha hadn't pulled away yet. She knew there was some truth to Sasha's words, but Dani still spent her nights trying to find a way where she could save both of them, torturing herself with the thought that if she was just stronger or smarter, it would have been possible.

Sasha forced her gaze down, forced her out of that cycle, with a gentle tilt of her chin. 'Do you honestly think Eve would want you to keep punishing yourself?'

Dani shook her head, because there was nothing left to say.

'It wasn't your fault,' Sasha said again. 'You

can't carry this around for ever. You deserve to forgive yourself.'

Dani pressed a kiss into Sasha's hair, the tears finally falling in rivulets. She'd been holding them back so long that they were impossible to stop—but Sasha was there to tell her it was okay. To kiss her until it hurt a little less.

And maybe she did feel lighter come morning knowing that the weight was no longer a secret. That Sasha knew the worst parts of her, and chose to wake up in her arms anyway.

CHAPTER TWENTY-TWO

SASHA MOVED THROUGH the town with a new spring to her step the following morning, an unbridled smile on her face that remained as long as her hand was in Dani's. She hadn't expected to find this much happiness so soon after her Hollywood exit, let alone with someone so rooted in the real world. Someone so strong and loving and brave, even if Dani refused to see it for herself.

'What are you smiling about?' Dani quipped, though the corners of her own mouth were punctuated by gorgeous dimples that Sasha wanted to kiss. She wanted to kiss all of her. She'd made good headway last night, but there was still so much more left to discover. She already ached for them to be alone again.

Bashfully, she dipped her head into Dani's shoulder. 'Breakfast. Do I want pancakes or patatas bravas?'

'Or *churros*?' teased Dani.

Sasha stopped in the middle of the sandy path overlooking the beach to laugh and pull Dani closer. 'Right. Churros are an option now. At least we won't have to lie to Teo any more. Not that it was ever very hard to pretend I was…' *In love with you*, she'd almost said, but bit down on her tongue to stop the words from pouring out. She'd made enough grand confessions of adoration last night, and she was frightened of coming off too strong. Frightened Dani might still change her mind, even if she hadn't crept away at dawn like last time.

Dani placed her hands on either side of the railing behind Sasha, Sasha's spine arching over the top pole as their stomachs pressed together. 'Pretend you were what? Annoyed at me for not liking breakfast food?'

A thrill fluttered through Sasha at their proximity, out in the open for everyone to see.

'Something like that,' she whispered. And then, because last night's performance was still on her mind, her brow furrowed. 'I was thinking that maybe I can trust Teo with the truth. I'm so tired of the lies, Dani. He doesn't even know my real name.'

Dani bristled, rocking back to put distance between them again as she deliberated. 'I don't know, Sash. Couldn't you wait a couple more weeks?'

Sash. That was new. Sasha liked it, just as she liked how serious Dani became whenever they spoke about her safety.

'I could…' She worried at her lip, and Dani finished her sentence for her.

'But you don't want to.'

'Last night was the first time I've felt *real* in a long time. No one was telling me what to do or how to do it. Teo was a big part of that. But I still feel like I'm in a cage, somehow, just a bigger one than before. I want to be myself. I want people other than you to know what that looks like. I want—'

Her heart began to racket against her ribs like a ping-pong ball at the sight beyond Dani's shoulder: a man pointing his bulky camera right at her on a zoomed lens. 'I want to know why that man is taking pictures of us.'

Dani whipped around in a blur, shoulders squaring immediately as she eclipsed Sasha from the photographer's view.

'Sasha! Why have you been hiding in Spain?' the man called in a heavy French accent. 'Is it true you disappeared from the Sara Chase movie set without telling anybody?'

The ground beneath Sasha's feet cracked open, debris crumbling all around her. This couldn't be happening. They couldn't have found her already. How—?

'Why are you performing in local dive bars when you should be working, Sasha?' another voice piped up from her left.

Of course. Paparazzi travelled in flocks, like

vultures. Sasha wound her fingers into Dani's shirt, head spinning as she tried to catch a full breath. She couldn't. Her muscles locked, stomach cramping.

Dani had been right. She should have stayed at home last night. Every night. Only then would she ever escape this.

Across the road, by the stall of musical instruments, Teo was a blurred, familiar face among a steadily growing sea of onlookers. He shoved through the photographers, mouth moving, but Sasha couldn't understand a word over the piercing sirens in her ears.

It was over. This little bubble she'd been floating inside had popped.

Dani turned around, her chiselled mask of calm concern the one thing that Sasha could rely on. She took Sasha's hand, cupping her cheek with the other. 'Deep breaths, love. We're going to head to the cafe over there, okay? All you need to do is hold onto me.'

'I thought I could just have one night—' Sasha's voice was thick with tears, high-pitched with raw panic.

Dani shushed her softly, pressing a kiss between Sasha's brows before she could dissolve into the most broken version of herself. She couldn't feel her knees, wasn't sure how they were still holding her up.

'I'll get you out of this, and you'll have as many

nights as you want. Here.' She slipped off her sunglasses and put them on Sasha, then tugged her into her body. Sasha clamped her arms around Dani's torso with a whimper, squeezing her eyes shut when the camera flashes grew more intense.

Teo led them across the road, but it only got worse, the paparazzi trailing closer—as though their movement gave them permission to invade.

'Sasha, have you been living a double life?'

'What's with the new haircut?'

'Are you pregnant? Is it Tom's baby?'

Sasha flinched when a hand yanked at her arm, and then Dani's vicious snarl bled through the white noise. *'Back off!'*

Something slammed at Sasha's feet, and she dared peel her eyes open to see a camera smashed against the flagstones. The photographer began shouting in French, but Dani was louder. Stronger. *Angrier.* 'Don't touch her again, you sick scumbag!' And then, as though she'd never been angry at all, she said softly, 'I've got you. We're almost there now.'

It didn't matter where they were. This was Sasha's life. It would *always* be Sasha's life, until she was picked apart and there was nothing left.

Not even Dani could hold her together this time.

A group of bewildered patrons were ushered out of the cafe by a short, dark-haired woman who

Teo introduced as Elena. Dani planted Sasha on the nearest chair as the door was locked, shouts of the paparazzi finally muffled.

Crouched in front of Sasha, Dani took her hand again, the feather-light touch breaking through Sasha's spreading numbness.

'So, er, that was a little wild.' Teo pulled off his cap to rake back his flattened curls.

'Thank you for helping us,' Dani said, glancing between him and Elena. 'We weren't expecting it.'

Elena wiped her hands nervously on her coffee-stained apron, eyes wide. 'You are Sasha March.'

Sasha almost flinched at the name, the scrutiny. Instead, she only nodded.

'Everybody was talking this morning about how you performed in Santi's last night. I didn't believe them until they showed me the video.'

'Can I see it?' Dani beckoned, leaving no room for argument. Clumsily, Elena reached into her pocket and retrieved her phone, scrolling for a moment before handing it over. Sasha didn't want to look, but she heard it all the same: a recording of her and Teo singing, just as Dani had predicted would happen.

Sasha had been so foolish. She'd thought that being here, looking different, made her immune to their attention.

As though pretending enough would make this new life real.

She glimpsed the screen long enough to see that the video came from an Instagram reel with ten thousand likes and counting.

'Do you know the person who posted this?' Dani asked.

Elena nodded. 'A little.'

'Could you ask them to take it down?'

'It doesn't matter,' Sasha said.

But Dani didn't seem to hear her, standing up to return Elena's phone. 'As soon as possible. This needs to be deleted.'

'It doesn't matter!' Sasha erupted and then hugged her arms around herself. 'It's over, Dani. They already know I'm here. It's all over. And you were right. I shouldn't have performed. I shouldn't have thought it would be different this time.'

'Samantha…' Teo uttered gently.

'*Sasha.* My name is *Sasha*. I lied to you, Teo! In fact, I lie to everyone, all the time. Everything I am is a lie, because I'm not good enough for Hollywood as I am, but I don't belong here, either.' The words puddled out of her without any semblance of control, quivering with all the pain she'd been holding onto for so long. She wished she were still in Kent, busking on the streets. She'd been broke and alone, but at least she'd known privacy. At least she'd been free.

'Hey.' Dani knelt again, squeezing Sasha's knee. 'You deserve better than this. You'll *have* better than this. We can get away again. We can go anywhere you want. But they won't stop following you, and you know that. You need…' She sighed. 'You need to put an end to this properly. People expect an explanation, and I don't think they'll leave you alone until you give one. You can't keep running away for ever. It'll only end like this again.'

Sasha reared back, the words an insult despite Dani's soft tone. It sounded an awful lot as though Dani was blaming her. Calling her a coward. Didn't that make her a hypocrite?

'Do you *really* want to talk to me about running?' Sasha shouted. 'All you've done is run! From what happened to Eve, from me, from that award you don't think you deserve!'

Dani faltered, hurt flickering in her eyes. Sasha knew she'd regret it later, but now she was suffocating. Now she was losing herself all over again.

That became especially clear when Dani's mouth pressed into a thin, unforgiving line. She shifted over to the door like an obedient guard, her back turned against them.

Fighting back tears, Sasha looked at the marbled ceiling, slumping back into her chair. Teo's eyes were all sympathy, but even he looked too afraid to move closer.

'What is it you want?' he asked gently. 'What were you hoping to find?'

'A life free of what's outside,' Sasha admitted,

batting a hand at the crowd of photographers waiting for her to emerge. 'I just wanted… I wanted it all to stop. I'm sorry I lied to you and got you all wrapped up in this.'

'I mean, people know about my band now. I'm not complaining.' His smirk was wry. 'If last night was any indication, you are more than capable of going after what you want. I do not know you as Sasha March, although her songs on the radio are quite good.'

She almost smiled.

'I know you as the friend who is happy and full of life,' he continued. 'The friend who lives and breathes music, like me. Those fools out there cannot take that from you unless you let them.'

It wasn't nearly that simple, but Teo's words still sparked a flame of new defiance in her. He was right. She couldn't keep living her life skirting around people who didn't respect her. Perhaps it was time Sasha started to protect herself, instead of expecting someone else to do it for her.

She rubbed the tears from her eyes finally and said, 'I think I have to go back to Saint-Tropez.'

CHAPTER TWENTY-THREE

DANI HAD DIPPED out of the cafe's back entrance to usher Sasha out with as few witnesses as possible, but the villa's security cameras still showed scatterings of loiterers outside the gates. Their ruthlessness made Dani sick, more so when she thought of how persistent they'd been in town. The awful things they'd shouted, the way they'd tried to grab Sasha as if she were a rag doll to be picked up and played with.

Worse than that was the way Sasha had thrown last night's confessions back in Dani's face. *All you've done is run! From what happened to Eve, from me, from that award you don't think you deserve!*

Dani's protection hadn't been enough. Again, she'd endangered someone, too distracted by her feelings for her. History repeating itself, despite all the ways she'd tried to avoid it. If she were better at her job, capable, deserving, she never would have let Sasha sneak out to that bar.

She was nothing more than a failure, and Sasha was better off without her.

Cold seeped into her. She had to stop this. Now.

She picked up her phone and dialled Marcus's number.

Dani packed methodically, trying to find calm finality in the rhythm of folding her clothes, though her fingers shook, and eventually she piled them in without thought. When she was done, she waited with her bag at the bottom of the stairs, tidying up any signs they'd been here at all: clearing away the life they'd been creating together. The villa was as empty as though they'd never existed by the time Sasha came down, tear-stricken face hidden behind sunglasses and a cap. When she tried to kiss Dani, Dani turned to fidget with the zip on her bag.

'You're upset with me,' Sasha said.

'Are you ready to go?'

Silence as Sasha weighed her up, tugging off her sunglasses to look at her properly. 'Don't. Don't do this again. You promised you wouldn't push me away this time.'

She put her hand on Dani's arm, but Dani yanked it away in barely concealed ire. 'Dani,' Sasha begged.

It pierced through Dani's resolve. 'We can't do this any more.'

Sasha took a pained step back. 'You're going to give me the same speech again? Seriously?'

'I talked to Marcus. He's going to send you

a replacement who'll meet us in Saint-Tropez.' Dani tried to keep her voice from cracking as the finality hit her. They'd only just found each other, and now it had to be over. Dani had given parts of herself she'd never allow anyone else to see, and it had all been a mistake. A careless, silly mistake. She grabbed her bags, but Sasha dropped her own.

'Are you *kidding* me?' The question left her in a gut-wrenching sob.

One Dani tried, desperately, to ignore. 'Are you ready to go?'

'No,' snapped Sasha.

Dani cocked her head. 'What do you mean, *no*?'

'You don't get to turn this on and off!' Sasha's devastated voice scraped off the walls in echoes, and Dani could do nothing but hide the wince as it wracked through her. 'Either you want me, or you don't.'

'If you truly think it's that simple, you're naiver than I thought.' Dani barely recognised the frost in her own words. That easy way of disconnecting still surprised her, even now. A coping mechanism she'd clung onto, from the very first time she'd realised that she wasn't enough for her mum, through her father's funeral, and then Eve's. Overcompensating for her weakness, she knew, but she could think of no better way of handling this much hurt.

For that reason, Dani could never give Sasha what she wanted. As long as they were together, falling, she couldn't provide stability, because Sasha made *her* unstable.

She ruined her, as Dani had known she would. That made her a danger to Sasha, not a protector.

'Is this because of what I said in the cafe?' Sasha questioned. 'The thing about running? Because that's what you're doing! You're running, again, because you're scared—'

'I'm running because I can't keep doing this!' Dani erupted. 'Look at us, Sasha. It doesn't work! It was wrong of me to ever pursue this.'

'Don't say that. Nothing about the two of us is wrong!'

Wood cut into Dani's palms as she curled her hands around the edge of the table, grip so tight she imagined it might splinter. What did she have to do to make Sasha see? 'You're reckless. Impulsive. *Selfish.*'

Sasha flinched again, the colour leaching from her face.

'You deserve to be, after what you've been through,' continued Dani. 'But it's pretty clear I can't keep you safe, not with all these boundaries blurred, so you're going to get someone who can, and you're going to live the life you want, and I'm not going to be part of it, because I *can't* be.'

Finally, she saw understanding dawn, twisted tightly with the sting of rejection. She deserved better. Dani convinced herself that, with her out of the picture, Sasha would *have* better.

'We could be together now,' Sasha rasped weakly. 'If there's a replacement, if your job isn't at risk any more, you could be with me. But…you don't want to be, do you? You never saw a future beyond this. I was just your job.'

Maybe Sasha was right. Dani wasn't willing to put her heart on the line for something that was born from the thrill of forbidden, unexpected lust. Something that could so easily slip through her fingers like the last person she'd loved, whether it was because of the danger or because Sasha was a livewire, made to walk her own path.

They hadn't been thinking clearly. They'd lost themselves in the sun and the luxury and the hiding. That didn't make for a steady long-term relationship.

It made for the same disasters Dani had faced once before.

'Did you really expect me to give everything up for you? Do you truly not see how incompatible we are?' Dani retorted. 'You're right. This—the fame, the glamour—isn't my life. It's my *job*, and I can't even do that right.'

The silence that followed felt like needles across Dani's skin. With bloodshot eyes and hunched shoulders, Sasha looked like the woman she'd been when they'd met, defeated by the world. Only, then, Dani had been the one to pull her out of it, not the one to sink her even further.

'You're right,' Sasha decided finally, chin wobbling as she moved to look out of the window. 'I expected too much from you.'

Dani should have felt vindicated to have got through to Sasha, but she only felt broken.

She picked up Sasha's bag and held it out, glaring at the photographers outside. 'It's not the right time to do this. We need to go.'

Sasha sniffled, grabbing the bag. 'I'm going. But not with you. Teo's still waiting outside. I'll have him take me to the airport.'

'Look at it out there.' Dani jabbed a finger at the window. 'For once, Sasha, stop being so ridiculous. Let me get you to Saint-Tropez first.'

'I don't need you to get me anywhere!' Sasha shouted. Dani rocked on her heels, the wind knocked out of her. 'Maybe I've relied on you too much, but I need to do this without you. Go home. Tell Marcus the work is done and I'm with your replacement. I'll tell him you did an excellent job and we'll all move on.'

She was already hooking her arms around the straps of her backpack. When she stepped towards the door, Dani's fingers curled around Sasha's arm. The thought of her going out there alone left her nauseous. She didn't care whether they were fighting. She didn't care if she'd made a terrible mess of things. She didn't care if Sasha had finally had enough. She wasn't leaving without her. 'Stop it. Now. You *know* it's not safe.'

'I don't want to see you again!' Sasha shouted, ripping her arm away. 'You want to push me away? Congratulations. You have. Now let me go.' She left without so much as a final glance, slamming the door behind her. Dani's instinct was to run after her, but when she got outside, Sasha was already scrambling into Teo's car against the onslaught of a restless, greedy audience, and Dani knew it would only stoke more fire if she followed. She'd be making it worse for them both.

And besides, that hollow finality in Sasha's voice had torn something in Dani. A strength she'd taken for granted until now. She went back inside and closed the door behind her, throat filling with bile when the first thing she saw was the guitar case.

Sasha had left this life behind.

Dani sank to the floor and wondered if she'd be able to do the same.

CHAPTER TWENTY-FOUR

NOTHING ABOUT SAINT-TROPEZ had changed in Sasha's absence, the film set still teeming with professionals like a well-oiled machine. They'd never needed her. She hoped that meant they'd let her leave quietly.

She used her ID to make it through the gates and was unsurprised when Rafael and Tom appeared in a cart before she'd even made it to the offices, chauffeured by a production crew member they likely didn't even know the name of.

Sasha's knees threatened to buckle, but she kept her head high as she waited for them to get out of the cart to greet her. It was Tom she faced first, and she already found it easier than she might have a fortnight ago. Whatever feelings she'd had for him once were built on faux charm and a naive longing for love, not the hurricane Dani had swept her into. He didn't deserve her submission.

Still, for extra courage, she imagined Dani at her back, muttering reassurances, because, somehow, she'd always known the right things to say even without saying much at all. The thought of her sent a wash of pain through Sasha, but that comfort hadn't ebbed even now. Even when Sasha might never see her again. She'd already dismissed her replacement, informing him and Marcus that their services were no longer needed.

The promise of loneliness that lingered when all this was done didn't feel nearly as scary as it used to. At least now she had her music. She'd go back to Spain, enjoy her new friendships and try not to think too much about Dani's absence. She deserved better than her constant rejection, anyway.

'Our little runaway returns. It was only a matter of time,' Tom drawled, oily gaze scraping up and down her figure. He wrinkled his nose, pinching the flimsy material of her simple yellow sundress with derision. 'What the hell are you wearing?'

She didn't have time to reply. Gabriella emerged from one of the offices behind, heels clicking harshly against the concrete as she approached. Her dark ponytail swung behind her shoulders like a pendulum. 'Well, if it isn't Sasha March. I was about to drag you back from Spain myself, but I'm glad to see you saved me the job. I hope you've already booked a hair appointment.'

'You'd better have a good explanation about why you swanned off my set for a fortnight, darling,' said Rafael coolly. 'Do you have any idea the money and time we've lost, waiting for you? We were about to recast you!'

'Good. You should.' Sasha snatched her dress away from Tom before his greedy hands climbed any further up her thighs. 'I'm sorry that I wasn't brave enough to tell you in person, but I have no intention of working with any of you again.'

The condescension in Gabriella's smirk made Sasha's skin crawl. 'You selfish little brat. I've given you *everything*.'

'You also *took* everything,' snapped Sasha. 'You cut me into pieces and reshaped me into somebody I don't recognise. You replaced my songs with someone else's. You told me every day that I'd only be good enough if I survived on diets and smiles, if I did everything that was asked of me, no matter what it cost. You erased me and replaced me with your idea of perfect, only that still wasn't enough, because there's always more money to make and pounds to lose and trends to follow. All I am to you is a prop, and I'm done with it, Gabriella.'

Rafael whistled through his teeth. 'Look, clearly you are experiencing some kind of mental break—'

Sasha interrupted: '*No.* I'm grateful for the opportunities you gave me, Rafael, but I don't belong here.'

'You see, Raf,' Tom said, glare scathing, '*this*

is why we didn't work. Always making such a big deal out of nothing.'

'You still have a contract to uphold,' said Gabriella, 'or did you forget that on your little impromptu vacation?'

'You can take that up with my lawyer,' she said, only to Rafael. 'This is the last time any of you will see me. I'll make an announcement tonight that I'm leaving Hollywood to focus on my well-being, and then that will be it.'

'And what about when you get bored and lonely in two months' time?' Tom quipped. 'I know you. You're like a whiny little rescue puppy. You *need* attention.'

'You *don't* know me,' she whispered. 'Not at all.'

It wasn't attention she'd craved from him. It had been what he'd promised in his vows: love. She wouldn't keep being made to feel like the pathetic one for expecting him to follow through, though she'd admit she should have known long ago that he was incapable of anything close to the sentiment.

'I'll make your life hell,' Gabriella warned, already clutching her phone in her hand. The fear of having Sasha's reputation tattered was nothing more than a dull glimmer now. She'd find her way through it. The people worth keeping around wouldn't care about who Hollywood thought she was. 'By this time tomorrow, your name will be tarnished like every other client who has gone behind my back.'

'And that's why I won't do this, Gabriella. I don't want my career to be built on your manipulation. You can't control me any more.'

Gabriella grabbed Sasha's wrist, her false nails biting into flesh so tightly Sasha had to trap a whimper. 'This is your last chance.'

The wild, vicious glint in Gabriella's inky eyes was proof it was she who needed Sasha, not the other way around. Her livelihood depended on artists like Sasha. Without her biggest pop sensation, who was she?

Just a cold-hearted puppeteer lacking her marionettes. Sasha hoped, one day, she might be able to change things. Talk to Gabriella's other clients, help them see that it didn't have to be this way. Nobody deserved an agent who wanted to tear them down.

For now, she needed to get out—on her terms, without hiding. She could deal with the fallout as long as she no longer owed anything to anyone. Maybe she'd even be brave, confess about the mistreatment she'd faced so that fans knew just what sort of star-studded industry they were supporting. Most people would choose not to believe her, as they so often did when it came to women especially, but some might listen. Some might *see*.

For the first time, she could see a future where

she didn't have to either submit or run. She'd own this part of her life to help pave a better one. She'd release music she wanted to hear, and she wouldn't care how many listened.

She would never, ever surround herself with people who wanted to drag her down again.

You deserve better than this, Dani had said. *You'll* have *better than this.*

She wanted better. Maybe Dani was right and they weren't meant to be, but Sasha still saw glimmers of red hair and swirling tattoos in the future she was imagining. She was so tired of being the only one to want it. The only one to fight for them.

'Thank you for the opportunities,' Sasha said, gaze snagging on each of them in turn. 'I'm sorry it had to come to this, but I'm not prepared to sell any more parts of myself to keep you all happy. All I ever wanted was to make music and stay true to my own voice. And you're right, Tom, I did want to be loved. Now I see I was looking in the wrong places.'

Rafael marched off first, already pressing his phone to his ear and snapping, 'Can we see how available Jennifer Lawrence currently is?'

Gabriella's claws finally lifted from Sasha's skin as she sneered down her nose. 'You were nobody when I met you. I made you somebody.'

'No, Gabriella. You made me a commodity. It isn't the same thing.' But Gabriella would never see that. She thrived off the material, and, worse, she knew how to chip away at her clients until they felt as though she was all they had, which was why she'd always succeed here.

'Stupid girl,' she said, and then was gone, too.

Only Tom was left, still with that arrogant little smirk on his lips. This meant nothing to him. If anything, Sasha was just another source of entertainment. A story he'd laugh about over dinner tonight. She was okay with that. 'You know, I really don't know what I ever saw in you.'

'Likewise,' Sasha gritted out.

He snickered at her a final time, and then she was left alone.

Free.

As exhilarating as it was, she walked out of the gates not knowing what came next.

The cage was gone, but Sasha was still alone. And, worse, she was heartbroken for the only person who had ever felt safe.

CHAPTER TWENTY-FIVE

DANI WAS STILL crumpled on the floor when Teo buzzed in through the villa's gates hours later. When he opened the door, he let out a series of lamenting tuts on her behalf. 'Danielle.'

'Dani.' Her correction was sharper than intended.

He made a show of surrender and slid onto the floor across from her.

'She made it okay?' Dani couldn't help herself: she needed to know Sasha was safe, even now.

'Yes, but she didn't tell me why *I* was taking her instead of you.'

'I had to let her go.' Dani's voice cracked, and she cleared her throat quickly, hoping he hadn't heard—but the sympathy swirling in his eyes said she wasn't that lucky. 'We weren't really together, so stop looking at me like that. I was hired to protect her. She came up with the dating act because she thought you'd ask fewer questions.'

'It didn't seem like an act from over here.' Teo nudged Dani with his foot. 'It's not too late to fix it.'

She scoffed. 'Yes, it is. I can't ignore all the ways we don't work. She's about to get the freedom she's always wanted, and I…' Dani dipped her head, sinking further against the weight of the truth.

'You?' Teo cocked his head expectantly. Dani had forgotten she'd even been talking. Usually, she was better at keeping it all in, but it was as though last night had unlocked her right down to her darkest corners. Changed, all because Sasha had listened to her story and accepted her without judgement.

'I don't belong in her life,' she said finally. 'I'm like…a flat tyre on her Mercedes-Benz.'

'Whoa. Can I write that down for a lyric?'

She glared, and Teo gave a withering grimace. 'Sorry.'

She didn't even know why she was bothering. He was hardly going to solve her relationship troubles, if Dani could even call their brief stint a relationship. The best thing she could do now? Go back to London and accept her new job role. She'd tried to force herself up multiple times, but her legs were stuck in quicksand. Leaving the villa meant it was really over. She'd lose something she'd only just found, something she hadn't wanted to let go of.

'Well, I saw no flat tyres,' Teo continued tentatively. 'If anything, the two of you are like fireworks when you're together—and sad little ashes when you're not.'

'You're terrible at this pep-talk thing,' Dani muttered.

'Is it not true?'

She rested her elbows on her knees. Yes, it might be true that she currently felt like 'sad little ashes', without light and warmth for the first time since she'd met Sasha. But she wouldn't always. She'd move on. Eventually.

She just wasn't sure she wanted to. When they'd been together, their future had been a distant, indefinite thing. Dani had felt as though she had all the time in the world to memorise Sasha's laugh, her body, her lips. Their argument didn't feel like a goodbye, and Dani wouldn't be able to even think of moving from this floor until she knew if Sasha was safe—which she only would when she got back to the office, because she had no way of contacting her otherwise.

Dani tipped her head back, closing her gritty eyes before tears could fall. She was past being able to filter her thoughts now. Who cared what Teo thought of her? Who cared about her at all?

Nobody. Sasha March was the only person in the world she'd opened up to, even if only for a moment in time, and the knowledge of it left loneliness weeping out of every corner of her. So she spoke. To the wrong person, maybe, but she needed to put all of this hurt somewhere. To sort out her thoughts into something she could make sense of so that she could stop moping and get up.

'I used to think that I was meant to do something good, y'know. I joined the police to help people. Then my dad died, and it was like I saw death everywhere. Diving for people who were already gone wasn't heroic; it was just sad. And then I lost Eve, and all I could focus on was how badly I'd wished it were me. It was *my* fault.' The tears slipped past her lashes anyway, and she let them. For once, she let them. 'She was right. I *was* running from what happened. I couldn't face going back to the police, so I pretended that providing security for well-off people was a decent career move. And it is. But it isn't something I ever wanted. Certainly not something my dad would want for me. And it doesn't make me feel like I'm atoning for my mistakes. It makes me feel like I'm hiding from them. That was enough before. I didn't have anything left to lose.'

'But now, you have Sasha to lose,' said Teo gently.

She nodded. 'And I've lost her. I proved I wasn't capable enough to protect her. I never am.'

He shuffled closer, putting a hand on Dani's knee. 'I saw the opposite. The way you guarded her from that mob today wasn't just professional. It was fierce. And the way she leaned into you wasn't just something she needed. It was something she *wanted*. She told me that those songs she sang at Santi's were about you. That she hasn't had anything to sing about for so long until *you*. You are the only person who doesn't see how wonderful you are for her.'

Dani wanted so badly to believe it was true, but she had been left with nothing once before. She couldn't do it again.

Could she?

'Do you honestly think she's better with a stranger who does not know her struggles?' Teo continued. 'A stranger who, by the way, she's already planning to fire the second she gets to Saint-Tropez.'

Of course. That stubborn woman could never make it easier.

That was just one of the many reasons Dani loved her.

Thinking of Sasha back in that world, alone and hurting, left fear rattling through Dani. She had every right to handle it alone, and if she wanted to, Dani would let her. But she still deserved somebody to be there when it was done.

Nobody had been there for Dani after Eve. Not until last night.

It was time to face the truth: she wasn't the type of woman willing to sit on the floor and watch the thing she wanted pass by—or, at least, she didn't used to be, before her grief. If she wanted to be deserving of Sasha, she'd have to stop pushing her away for long enough to tell her how she really felt. She'd been trapped in the past for so long, but now it was the future that was holding her back.

She would go to Saint-Tropez to make sure Sasha was safe, and to give her the truth she'd been too afraid to admit. If Sasha didn't want her, then Dani would fight her way out of all this darkness the way she had before. She could go and see her aunt further down the coast, start being a real person again and not just a ghost in everybody else's life.

As long as she didn't stay like this, helpless and discontent.

She stood up, and Teo grinned. 'Would you perhaps like a lift to the airport?'

Dani picked up her bag, and then Sasha's guitar, because she couldn't start her new life without the thing she loved most. 'I could drive there myself, but I have a feeling you're quite enjoying this.'

'Oh, I am,' said Teo.

As much as Dani scoffed, secretly, she was grateful for his unexpected friendship. Perhaps she'd even tell him so on the journey, because opening up, apparently, was something she needed to work on.

Well, Dani was finally trying.

CHAPTER TWENTY-SIX

SASHA LOOKED OUT on the marina, a new uncertainty muddying her triumph. After a long call with her lawyer, she'd posted her announcement on all her social media accounts using the laptop she'd left behind in her villa, and then logged out—for good. Now a few tourists snapped not-so-subtle pictures of her, whispering her name, but she tried to ignore them. The sunset wasn't worth missing.

Besides, she was lost in thoughts of what came next. She found herself eager to return to Teo and the town she was slowly growing to love. Maybe she'd be brave and stop through a couple of different places first, see the world without lights and cameras, but with the chatter growing louder at her back, she wasn't sure she was ready to stop hiding away completely. With time, the chaos would die down, but her announcement would only spark more questions from the press, and she was half expecting the usual band of photographers to roll up any minute.

A couple was silhouetted on one of the yachts,

kissing with the sun rays flaring between them, and Sasha looked away with a noise of discomfort. Better not to be reminded of what she'd lost.

God, she already missed Dani, and it was stronger than any fear or anger or happiness she'd experienced in the last few weeks. The thrum under her veins whispered her name. Sasha would give anything to kiss her for the first time again.

'I can always find you by the sea, eh?'

For a moment, Sasha thought her desires had turned into fully fledged hallucinations, because that voice sounded an awful lot like Dani's. She turned around, pulse spiking despite the fact she was clearly going mad and Dani couldn't possibly be here—

Except she was, painted golden by the bright sky, hair a tangled, ruby mess atop her head and a bottle of champagne in her hand. She'd forgotten her sunglasses again, wrinkles deepening at the corners of her eyes as she stepped closer. Her free hand gripped the handle of Sasha's guitar case.

'You… You're here,' Sasha breathed.

'I'm here,' Dani replied. 'Couldn't let you go without this.' She set the case down by Sasha's feet, but Sasha barely looked at it. As much as she loved the instrument she'd poured her heart into for the last couple of weeks, it was the woman in front of her who stole all of her attention.

Dani waved the champagne bottle. 'And I heard congratulations are in order. Had some time to kill on the flight and saw you'd made the announcement. Good riddance, Hollywood.'

'Why are you…?' Sasha batted her lids to make sure she wasn't dreaming. 'Dani…' She needed to say her name just to make it feel real, and because it sounded as good as any song on her tongue.

'I understand if you never want to see me again,' Dani said. 'But I had to make sure you were okay. Not because it's my job, but because it's all I want: for you to be okay.' She shifted, looking down at the mosaic floor beneath her.

'I thought you'd already be back in London,' Sasha admitted.

'Suppose I'm not that easy to get rid of, either.' Dani gave a lopsided smirk. Sasha wished she could return it, but every fibre of her was trying to protect herself from more hurt. Dani being here meant another goodbye would be coming soon, if not today, then tomorrow.

She frowned. 'Aren't you expected back at work?'

'No.' Dani shrugged as though it was the simplest thing in the world. 'I quit.'

'Why?' Sasha spluttered.

'You were right. I was using it to escape everything that happened with Eve. I always wanted to help people, but you're the first client who I felt like I was actually making a difference with. I'd missed that feeling. It was why I joined the police in the first place, but, after everything I lost, I didn't think I could be trusted to do that any more.'

Sasha's fingers danced at her sides, restless with the urge to reach out and tell her over and over again until she finally saw it. 'So, you're going to go back to Yorkshire?'

'I don't know.' Dani finally looked at her properly, eyes reflecting the yachts bobbing by the docks in shades of amber. 'That depends on you.'

'Me?' Sasha's voice wavered, a clamp tightening around her chest.

'If you still want me.'

She'd *always* want her, but… 'I mean, I won't need a bodyguard for much longer. I think I'm going to go back to Spain, play with Teo some more and see where it takes me.'

'I didn't mean as your bodyguard, Sash.' Dani's fingers ghosted over Sasha's wrist, and Sasha shivered against the balmy sea breeze. 'I'm sorry I messed it all up. I pushed you away because I was scared, and that wasn't fair.'

'Scared of what?' Sasha whispered. She thought she knew, but needed to hear it.

Tears glittered in Dani's eyes. 'How much I feel for you. I lost the only other woman I loved. It was my responsibility to protect her, and I failed, the same way I failed with you. I can't handle that kind of loss again, but it feels inevitable because… I don't think I deserve you, Sasha.'

Sasha's heart broke all over again. How was

it that Dani still didn't see how strong she was? That her one terrible moment of loss couldn't take away all the good in her?

'You're wrong. I understand that you went through something terrible, but it wasn't your fault. I'll tell you that as many times as you need to hear it.' Sasha cupped Dani's face, catching her tears as they finally fell. 'You never failed me. You never could. You're the strongest, most *infuriating* person I've ever met, and I wouldn't be here, finally safe and free, without you.'

She cleared the lump from her throat. 'I don't need you to feel responsible for me. I just need you to be in this with me.'

'I am. I'm in this. No more messing around.' Finally, Dani took her hands, spreading warmth back into Sasha's palms. 'I love you, and no matter what I've lost before, what I'm scared to lose again, I can't let you go.'

'Really?'

Dani nodded. 'Really.'

Sasha could hardly believe that this was the same woman who had pushed her away so many times. She was saying everything Sasha wanted to hear, and *this* was what she'd been chasing. Quiet and independence, yes, but also a love that was real and right, not something that just looked nice on magazine covers.

She fell into Dani's arms on weak knees, holding on tightly in case Dani tried to let go again.

Dani chuckled softly, drawing across Sasha's spine with a tenderness that radiated through every bone, every nerve.

When she pulled away, Dani traced the line of her jaw, placing a kiss on the tip of her nose, and then her damp lashes, her forehead, her neck, before finally finding her lips. People watched, took pictures, but neither of them cared, the rest of the world blurring into the background until Dani was all that there was. All that there'd ever been.

'You've turned me soft, Sasha March,' Dani whispered against her mouth.

Sasha smiled, her breath trembling out of her. She'd never felt a certainty quite like this, enough to make all of her doubts disappear. 'You've made me stronger, Dani Sharpe.'

Dani shook her head. 'You did that all on your own, love.'

But it wasn't all true. She wouldn't be here, kissing Dani in plain sight, if Dani hadn't reminded her that she deserved to live her life unapologetically. To take her autonomy back. To be herself again.

She curled her arms around Dani's neck and said, 'What now?'

'You tell me.'

Sasha was content to tuck herself into Dani's side and watch the sun set, knowing that, tomorrow, she'd ask the same question again.

They had plenty of time to decide on the answer.

EPILOGUE

DANI'S HAIR WAS still damp, muscles still in knots, from her long day at work, but she refused to let that deter her from the evening's plans. Romantic gestures were not her strong suit, but she had a ring in her pocket and a handful of candles, so, as she hauled her picnic basket onto the sand, she hoped that it would be enough.

For Sasha, nothing would ever *really* be enough. Dani still struggled to comprehend how she'd got lucky enough to find a love like theirs, and luckier still that they got to enjoy it in the place where it had all begun: Dénia, Spain. They'd moved into a smaller cottage closer to the seafront a few weeks back; as nice as the villa was, it was too big for the two of them, and here they were closer to work. Dani had got her lifeguard qualification and volunteered with Maritime Rescue, and Sasha helped Teo run his business now that his father had retired. The fast pace and glamour of their old lives had faded a while ago, allowing them to finally just *be*.

So, on the day of their first anniversary, Dani

couldn't think of any reason she shouldn't propose, even if the ring was far less remarkable than some of the jewellery tucked away in Sasha's old things.

From the bar across the road, she saw Sasha emerge with Teo and swore. She had approximately two minutes to lay out the blanket and candles—and, okay, rose petals, because she really was working on the romance thing—before Sasha saw her and likely guessed exactly what was going on. All Dani wanted was for it to be perfect. She muttered at the lighter to stop flickering out against the sea breeze, then scattered the petals and placed down the champagne she'd bought. She just hoped she didn't still smell like sweat and seaweed.

'What's this?'

Dani looked up, her heart pounding at the sight of Sasha being ushered onto the beach by Teo. Her pink skirt billowed in the wind, chestnut waves rippling in tandem. The most beautiful woman Dani had ever seen. Even after a year, it still surprised her how strongly her body reacted. It was different now. The fire between them still burnt hot, but there was also a calm Dani had never experienced before. At work, she was a live wire, cutting through the sea to make sure endangered swimmers and boaters weren't dragged under. With Sasha, all of that energy settled like silt at the bottom of a riverbed. She could relax, knowing she was safe and hers.

So, really, it didn't matter that half the candles had blown out and the petals were scattering across the sand. It didn't matter that Dani had forgotten the chocolate-covered strawberries, which she realised now with a disgruntled huff. It didn't even matter that seagulls scavenged overhead, squawking noisily for the contents of the picnic basket.

'Come here.' Dani beckoned, nerves rattling through her. She held her hand out, and Sasha took it, glancing around apprehensively.

'Did you do this?'

'Don't look so surprised. It's our anniversary. Wanted to make it special.'

Sasha smiled, all rosy cheeks and sparkling eyes. The pink clouds and dipping sun were unmissable, but they missed them, this time, to look at each other. Dani snaked her arms around Sasha's waist, and Sasha's hands clasped around the nape of Dani's neck. Slotting into place. Coming home.

'Wow. Dani Sharpe really has turned soft,' Sasha muttered teasingly.

'Yup. Only for you, love.'

'How was work?' Sasha's brows furrowed with concern as she twirled a damp strand of Dani's red hair around her finger. 'Did you find him?'

They'd been out with lifeboats, looking for a

boy who had fallen off his father's yacht, all afternoon. It was still difficult to face the water sometimes, but she did it—for Eve, for herself, for the people who needed her. It wasn't like it used to be. Now more lives were saved than lost. When they weren't, Sasha was always there at the end of the day to remind her that she'd done all she could. That she hadn't failed.

'We did. He's safe and sound,' Dani said softly. 'What about you? How's the album coming along?'

Sasha had taken over Teo's band as the lead vocalist after Raul's exit, and they'd already released a few covers to get fans excited. Many flocked to hear Sasha March's new songs—though she was known now by her real name, Sasha Marten—but their audience was much smaller, and Sasha had vowed that she'd keep it about the music. If the spotlight was on her, it would only be when she was playing, just as she'd wanted. And if the gigs got bigger, she'd joked that she had her personal bodyguard to take care of her, which was true. Dani's job might not have been to protect her any more, but she still did it fiercely.

'Good. We got a gig in Marbella this weekend. I thought maybe you could come, visit your aunt.' Sasha played with the buttons on Dani's loose black shirt.

Dani hummed, liking the sound of that. She'd finally reunited with Aunt Irene and her cousins last autumn, and they kept in contact regularly. It was nice to have a family again. Being alone had been easier than facing all the grief in her life, but Sasha had pulled her out of that self-sabotage in so many ways.

'Shall we sit?' Dani asked.

Sasha hitched up her skirt to make herself comfortable on the blanket. She placed her sandals by her side, admiring the basket of tapas Elena had thrown together. No time for cooking as planned, but the fluffy olive bread and cheeses were far more delicious anyway.

Dani went straight for the champagne, popping the cork with practised ease. She didn't miss the way Sasha licked her lips, focus lingering on Dani's tattooed arms.

'Eyes up here, Marten,' she quipped with a smug smirk.

Sasha batted her lashes. 'I'm only admiring your strength.'

The champagne fizzed as Dani poured them both a flute, and Sasha clinked her glass against Dani's. 'Happy anniversary, sweetheart.' She tsked. 'And you thought we wouldn't last.'

'I'm still trying to figure out why you put up with me,' Dani admitted, sinking closer as she sipped.

'The muscles, obviously.' Sasha jabbed her arm before placing a kiss on Dani's cheek. 'I love you.'

Dani's hands were clammy as she tugged the jewellery box from her pocket. 'I love you, too.

I never thought I could be this happy, but you… Well, you changed everything.'

When Sasha froze, blue eyes widening, Dani wondered if she'd made a mistake. Was it too much, too soon?

'Dani,' she whispered, fingers trembling against the stem of her glass. She set it down before the champagne sloshed over the rim, grazing a finger over the velvet box.

Dani flicked the lid open, the pear-shaped garnet winking against the sunset, and Sasha gasped. Tears filled her eyes.

'When we rocked up here a year ago today, we were both a little bit broken and lost,' Dani said, voice wobbling. 'You found me, Sasha. You were everything I didn't know I needed, and I couldn't ever let you go. I want to spend the rest of my life with you, here or anywhere else. I want to cheer for you at every show and see a million more sunsets with you. I want you to be my wife, if you've not had enough of me yet. So… I was wondering if you might like that, too. If you might like to marry me.'

The crashing waves were all that filled the silence for moments on end, and Dani held her breath, plagued with the fear that Sasha's answer would be no. She was still waiting for this whirlwind to end. In her world, the good things never lasted.

But then Sasha's face broke with a smile brighter than the sun, tears rolling down her cheeks. 'Of course I want to marry you!' She threw herself around Dani, peppering kisses all over her face. 'I could never have enough of you. You're the best thing that's ever happened to me. One of these days, you're going to realise that.'

'I'm getting there.'

Sasha choked on something that might have been a laugh or a sob, glancing down at the ring. 'Is that a garnet?'

'It seemed fitting.'

'It's so beautiful, Dan.'

'Glad you like it.' Dani plucked the ring from its case and slid it onto Sasha's finger, the red jewel made richer by Sasha's golden tan.

A frown puckered on Sasha's brows suddenly. Dani pressed her thumb against the wrinkle. 'What? What's wrong? Was this not…? Did I mess something up?'

'No, it's perfect. I just wanted to be the one to ask first,' Sasha admitted, leaning her forehead against Dani's as she cupped her jaw.

It sounded so silly that Dani snorted, tracing the shape of Sasha's summer freckles across the curve of her cheek. 'Clearly, I'm more eager than you.'

'No,' Sasha retorted sternly. 'I wasn't sure if you were ready. If it were up to me, I would have married you the day I met you.'

Dani was beginning to believe that, slowly. She pressed a soft kiss on Sasha's lips, and then another for good measure. 'You're happy, though?'

Sasha's fingers twisted through the hair at Dani's neck, always so tender. 'I've never been happier.'

It was all Dani had ever wanted, and she knew nobody who deserved it more.

'I love you, Sash. So much,' Dani said, struck by the truth of it even if she'd known it for a long time.

Sasha snuggled into her side as they watched the sun set together, nibbling at food and sipping champagne long after the sky darkened to a dusty blue. Later, in the dark, they would run into the water and remember the first time they'd touched one another, and Dani would try to memorise the taste of Sasha's skin all over again, even if it was a constant now.

This warmth in her chest wasn't just happiness, she knew. It was belonging. It was *knowing*. With or without the ring, she was Sasha's for ever—without barriers or obstacles, without fear. What was once an escape was now their haven, and Dani intended to keep it that way.

* * * * *

Bodyguard's Saint-Tropez Temptation
is Bryony Rosehurst's debut title for Harlequin Romance.

Visit the Author Profile page at Harlequin.com for more titles from Bryony Rosehurst.

Get up to 4 Free Books!

We'll send you 2 free books from each series you try PLUS a free Mystery Gift.

Both the **Harlequin® Historical** and **Harlequin® Romance** series feature compelling novels filled with emotion and simmering romance.

YES! Please send me 2 FREE novels from the Harlequin Historical or Harlequin Romance series and my FREE Mystery Gift (gift is worth about $10 retail). I may cancel anytime by emailing ReaderServiceInfo@Harlequin.com or by calling 1-800-873-8635. If I don't cancel, I will receive 5 new Harlequin Historical books every month and be billed just $6.39 each in the U.S. or $7.19 each in Canada, or 4 new Harlequin Romance Larger-Print books every month and be billed just $7.19 each in the U.S. or $7.99 each in Canada, a savings of 20% off the cover price. It's quite a bargain! Shipping and handling is just 75¢ per book in the U.S. and $1.75 per book in Canada.* I understand that accepting the free books and gift places me under no obligation to buy anything—they are mine to keep for free no matter what I decide.

Choose one: ☐ Harlequin Historical (246/349 BPA G3CD) ☐ Harlequin Romance Larger-Print (119/319 BPA G3CD) ☐ Or Try Both! (246/349 & 119/319 BPA G3CE)

Name (please print)

Address Apt. #

City State/Province Zip/Postal Code

Email: Please check this box ☐ if you would like to receive newsletters and promotional emails from Harlequin Enterprises ULC and its affiliates. You can unsubscribe anytime.

Mail to the **Harlequin Reader Service:**
IN U.S.A.: P.O. Box 1341, Buffalo, NY 14240-8531
IN CANADA: P.O. Box 603, Fort Erie, Ontario L2A 5X3

Want to explore our other series or interested in ebooks? Visit www.ReaderService.com or call 1-800-873-8635.

*Terms and prices subject to change without notice. Prices do not include sales taxes, which will be charged (if applicable) based on your state or country of residence. Canadian residents will be charged applicable taxes. Offer not valid in Quebec. This offer is limited to one order per household. Books received may not be as shown. Not valid for current subscribers to the Harlequin Historical or Harlequin Romance series. All orders subject to approval. Credit or debit balances in a customer's account(s) may be offset by any other outstanding balance owed by or to the customer. Please allow 4 to 6 weeks for delivery. Offer available while quantities last.

Your Privacy — Your information is being collected by Harlequin Enterprises ULC, operating as Harlequin Reader Service. For a complete summary of the information we collect, how we use this information and to whom it is disclosed, please visit our privacy notice located at https://corporate.harlequin.com/privacy-notice. Notice to California Residents—Under California law, you have specific rights to control and access your data. For more information on these rights and how to exercise them, visit https://corporate.harlequin.com/california-privacy. For additional information for residents of other U.S. states that provide their residents with certain rights with respect to personal data, visit https://corporate.harlequin.com/other-state-residents-privacy-rights.

HHHRLP2603